Irresistible Impulse

Irresistible Impulse

Vickie West

www.urbanbooks.net

Urban Books, LLC
114 Norman Ave.
Amityville, NY 11701

ISBN 13: 978-1-64556-757-8
EBOOK ISBN: 978-1-64556-758-5

First Trade Paperback Printing March 2026
Printed in the United States of America

10 9 8 7 6 5 4 3 2 1

Distributed by Kensington Publishing Corp.
Submit Orders to:
Customer Service
400 Hahn Road
Westminster, MD 21157-4627
Phone: 1-800-733-3000
Fax: 1-800-659-2436

The authorized representative in the EU for product safety and compliance
Is eucomply OU, Parnu mnt 139b-14, Apt 123
Tallinn, Berlin 11317, hello@eucompliancepartner.com

Irresistible Impulse

Vickie West

Chapter One

PRESS RELEASE: INTUITIVE ENERGY IS NAMED ONE OF AMERICA'S MOST INNOVATIVE COMPANIES AND ONE OF THE ONE HUNDRED BEST COMPANIES TO WORK FOR IN AMERICA.

However, in recent years, the stock price has been slipping. Tia Richards, who had led Intuitive for ten years, announced her retirement and was given a substantial severance package on her way out. In a move that shocked the energy industry, Savannah Ayers, who was a senior vice president for three years at BHV Power, was named president of Intuitive Energy. She will be the first person of color to head an energy company.

It was her first day in her new office with her new staff, and Savannah wanted to make a good first impression. That, of course, began with the look. *People see you before you get to speak a single word.* Consequently, her look needed to be on point to make a favorable first impression. It was going to be another hot Houston day; therefore, Savannah selected a bone Alexander McQueen sleeveless tailored suit.

When Savannah stepped off the elevator at eight o'clock and walked confidently into the offices of Intuitive Energy, she presented herself to Heather, the receptionist.

"Good morning, and welcome to Intuitive Energy. How can I help you today?"

"Good morning. My name is Savannah Ayers, and this is my first day here at Intuitive Energy."

"Oh, my."

Heather glanced at the time on her screen. Savannah was scheduled to arrive in the office at nine o'clock that morning. Brodrick Fowler, the chairman of the board at Intuitive Energy, had planned a welcome to the company, where he would make a grand speech because he liked to make grand speeches. Then he would walk Savannah around the floor, introducing her to key personnel in the company and any members of the board of directors who were in the building that morning. It was just after eight o'clock in the morning, and there she was.

"You're early."

"Yes. It's a habit of mine. Can you please let Mr. Fowler know I'm here? And if you could get somebody to show me to my office, I would truly appreciate it. What's your name?"

"Heather, Heather Strong." She quickly dialed the number of the admin pool. "I need somebody up here right now."

"Why? What's up?"

"She's here," Heather whispered.

"I am on my way."

"How long have you been working here, Heather?" Savannah asked when Heather got off the phone.

"Ten years."

"All of them as a receptionist?"

"No, ma'am—" Heather began, but Savannah cut her off.

"You call me ma'am again and today will end your ten-year career at Intuitive Energy. Please, call me Savannah or Ms. Ayers if you have to, but I am never ma'am." Savannah leaned forward. "Put the word out: don't call Savannah ma'am, or she'll fire you on the spot."

“I don’t know you well enough to know if you were serious or just having fun on your first day.”

“It’s a bit of both. I hate it when people my age call me ma’am. But I am just having fun with you, Heather. Put that out, too. She has a sense of humor.”

“Good morning, ladies,” a woman said as she walked up. “My name is Renee Maynard. I supervise the pool of administrative assistants here at Intuitive Energy.”

Savannah extended her hand. “Savannah Ayers. A pleasure to meet you, Renee. I was hoping you would be kind enough to show me to my office.”

Renee glanced at Heather because this wasn’t the plan. When she shrugged her shoulders, Renee pressed on.

“I will be happy to,” Renee said to Savannah. “If you would please follow me, I’ll show you to your new office. Might I be so bold as to welcome you to Intuitive Energy?”

“Thank you, Renee. It’s good to be here,” Savannah said, and Renee walked away from the receptionist’s desk.

As soon as they were gone from the area, Heather called Brodrick Fowler on his cell phone.

“Good morning, Heather. What can I do for you?”

“I was calling to let you know that Savannah Ayers is in the building.”

“Really? Early on her first day. That says a lot about who Savannah Ayers is and what kind of president she is going to be. Where is she now?”

“Renee Maynard is walking her to her office.”

Brodrick laughed. “I guess that’s how you get a brownnoser like Renee to get up out of her seat and walk somewhere other than the elevator when it’s time to leave.” Brodrick moved on, saving Heather from having to comment on Renee being a brownnoser or the implication that she was lazy. Both were true. “Do you know if they’ve installed the phone system in her office?”

"I don't know. But I will follow up with that department as soon as we hang up."

"Well, then I'm going to hang up so you can handle your business. I should be there in fifteen minutes."

"I will let Savannah know," Heather said.

"Getting a little chummy with the name of our new president, are we?"

"She said to call her Savannah or Ms. Ayers but never call her ma'am."

"Noted," Brodrick said, and he ended the call.

When Renee arrived at the corner office that was to be Savannah's office, she opened the door and found the phone ringing.

"I guess that's for me," Savannah said and walked into her new corner office. "Thank you for the escort, Renee."

"You're welcome," Renee said.

Savannah picked up the phone. "Savannah Ayers." No one was there, so she hung up.

Renee walked back to her section, wishing she had taken better advantage of the situation. She had just met the new president, and all she thought to talk about with her opportunity was the building's unique floor plan design, which Brodrick told her would foster teamwork and creativity. But she was spouting the company line, so she was on solid ground. Although Renee had no idea if she'd get another chance like that, she doubted it. Still, if another such opportunity arose, Renee would be ready with something better than the building's unique floor plan design.

Savannah went behind the desk and sat down. The chair wasn't very comfortable, so it had to go. She couldn't help but notice that there was no one in the office outside her door, where her assistant would be. Savannah wondered if that was because her assistant didn't come in until nine in the morning or because she would have the opportunity to interview and hire her own assistant. That would be her preference. Savannah would like to interview, hire, and most importantly, train her or him the way she needed to in order to do the things at Intuitive Energy that she wanted to do.

Even though she hadn't actually started working, she'd done quite a bit of research on Intuitive Energy before she allowed the headhunter to put her in for the position. Savannah had read about Tia Richards and the miraculous innovations that she brought to Intuitive Energy. She created a program that encouraged wholesale buyers of energy to purchase gas supplies and hedge the price risk at the same time. Tia began offering financing to oil and gas producers. It was under Tia Richards's leadership that a few changes to its business plan were implemented. Those few changes significantly improved the profitability of the company by investing in overseas assets.

Savannah saw the work put in by Tia Richards and thought that was why she was selected to be the new president over all the men who were also interested in the position. Perhaps their thinking was if a woman could create and implement those changes that made the company a powerhouse in the industry, hiring another woman with creativity was a good move. If that was their thinking, that was all right with her.

However, it is hard to follow a legend, and from what she read, Tia Richards was a legend. Now that she was in the building, she would find out if the people who worked with and for her felt the same way as the press.

Savannah spun around in her chair and looked at the view from her corner office. The view from the window was magnificent. "If nothing else, I'll enjoy the view."

"I sincerely hope you accomplish more than that while you're here."

The voice startled her but was familiar to her. When Savannah spun around, there stood Brodrick Fowler, the chairman of the board of Intuitive Energy.

"Good morning, Mr. Fowler. Please, come in and have a seat."

"First off, it's Brodrick." He sat down and smiled. "If you call me Mr. Fowler again, it will be the shortest tenure as president in the history of this company."

Savannah laughed. "I guess you talked to Heather?"

"I did."

"I was just having some fun with Heather. I hope she knows I wasn't serious."

"She knows now that you weren't serious, but at the moment, she wasn't quite sure."

"Do you think I need to speak with her to clear it up?"

"No."

"Good."

"So, I want you to know that you messed up my plans for this morning."

"How so?"

"By showing up here an hour early. When I came in, I was going to alert the security at the front door to make up some reasonable reason to not allow you into the offices. And at that point, I was going to come down and clear up the problem and escort you to the office. Then, I was going to make a 'welcome to Intuitive Energy' speech to the rank-and-file staff, who would have assembled while I was downstairs. Then, after my rousing and inspirational speech, you would say whatever it was that you wanted to say, and then we were going to take a tour of the building. I was going to introduce you to key members of management and some of the other key players. After that, I was going to make a big deal of bringing you here and showing you your corner office. But you messed that up, showing up for work early."

"I have made getting to places early a way of life. I've always found that it served me well because you do get to see things that you wouldn't see if I had gotten here at eight forty-five. And, just so you know, I would consider myself late getting here just fifteen minutes from the time I was scheduled to start."

"So, you'll be here early most days?"

"Most. I want to be arrogant and say I'll be here early every day, but this is my first day and I don't want to set the bar too high that even I can't reach it."

"A wise practice."

"Okay. How do we salvage the plans you had for today?"

"I've already taken care of that." Brodrick glanced at his watch. "As we speak, Heather is calling department heads and having them send people who aren't performing key functions within the company. She's going to send me a text message when she has assembled the troops for my speech and then yours."

"Okay. That sounds good. You can hang out in here until you get your text from Heather," Savannah said, and Brodrick stood up.

"I'll be in my office, and I'll come get you when they're ready."

"And where is your office?"

"I have the office at the other end of the hall. You can't miss it. Other than this office, mine is the only office on this hall."

"Just us."

"Just you and I, Savannah. My door is always open to you. And I expect you to use it. In order for this to work, you and I have to be in perfect tune. Walking the same walk, talking the same talk."

"I agree."

"I, like you, like to get in early. I'm generally here by eight. Why don't you and I meet in my office for coffee and snack cakes and sweets of every variety?" Brodrick smiled. "I like pastry."

"So do I. I am a sugar junkie. And I spend my share of time at the gym working it off. So, I will see you each and every morning at eight for coffee and snack cakes and sweets of every variety known to man."

Brodrick pointed at Savannah. "I knew I made the right decision."

"Before you go?"

"Yes."

"My assistant."

"You don't have one. I thought you should have the opportunity to interview and hire whomever you wanted, or if you wanted to hire your assistant at BHV away from them, that should be up to you."

"Thank you. That is exactly what I want. And yes, if I could bring my assistant over from BHV, that would be my preference. I'll speak with her today and gauge her interest in making the move."

"I'm sure she'll leap at the chance to make the move. Let me know as soon as you know," Brodrick said, and he left Savannah's office.

She picked up the phone and placed a call to Kiera Shields, who was her assistant at BHV.

"Good morning and thank you for calling BHV. This is Kiera Shields speaking. How can I help you this morning?"

"Hey, Kiera. How are you doing this morning?"

"I'm okay. I have no complaints."

"Miss me yet?"

"I do. Terribly." She lowered her voice. "The guy they brought in to replace you is an asshole. Where everybody loved you, it seems like he's trying his best to make everyone hate him."

"Then if I offered you a job here at Intuitive Energy, you would gladly accept and make the move?"

"Is that an offer?"

"Yes, Kiera. It is a real offer. I spoke with the chairman of the board. His name is Brodrick Fowler. I spoke with him about bringing you over. Actually, he was the one who suggested that if I wanted to bring you over, it would be all right with him." Savannah paused. "Or I could open it up, interview, hire, and train whoever I wanted. I told him what I want to do is continue to work with you."

"I wanna work with you, Savannah."

"Go on and give them a week's notice, and you can start here on Monday morning."

"Savannah, I am hanging up with you and typing my letter of resignation."

"We'll talk soon," Savannah said, and she placed the phone back in its cradle.

"Savannah Ayers?" asked the man standing in her doorway.

"Yes. How can I help you?"

"Actually, I came to help you get logged into the system. Bore you to tears while I update you on Intuitive Energy's computer use policy. Give you passwords. Show you how to change them."

Savannah pointed to him and smiled. "You're the IT guy."

He bowed. "Dylan Christensen at your service, Savannah. And yes, I spoke with Heather, so I know not to call you ma'am, and you prefer Savannah or Ms. Ayers. I prefer to call you Savannah since I have a feeling that you and I are gonna be buddies."

"I love my IT guys."

"I had that feeling the second I saw you," Dylan said and came around the desk. He pulled over a chair. "Okay. You ready to get started?"

"As long as you know that Brodrick Fowler may come to get me at some point, I'm ready."

"Yes, the 'welcome to Intuitive Energy' speech. I'm exempt from the meeting because I am deemed essential personnel. The people who have to come are . . . how did Debbie put it?"

"People who aren't performing key functions within the company?"

"Yes. How did you know? Oh, yeah, you're senior management."

"That and Brodrick told me about it."

"Right. Brodrick, the king of upper management." Dylan pointed to the computer. "May I?"

"Be my guest," Savannah said, and they switched seats.

Chapter Two

Once Dylan had finished doing everything that he needed to do with Savannah, he said goodbye only after she promised to call and ask for him specifically each and every time she was in need of IT support.

"You're my guy," Savannah promised.

She had just sat in the chair that had to go when Brodrick appeared in her doorway.

"You ready?"

"I am."

Savannah was excited to get started, so she bounced up, came from around the desk, and followed Brodrick to the elevator.

"Let me ask you a question."

"Fire away."

"The furniture in my office has to go. And I am talking especially about the chair. How do we make that happen?"

Brodrick chuckled as they continued walking to their elevator. "Sometime today, somebody in this building is going to show up at your door and present you with the corporate American Express black card. Go buy yourself the chair you want to sit in and the furniture you want to be surrounded by. I promise you, you are going to be spending a lot of time in that chair. You need to be comfortable in it. You are going to practically live in this office some days." He stopped and looked back at her. "And some nights. Feel free to decorate it any way you want."

Savannah saluted. "Yes, sir."

"By the way, Savannah. I feel the same way about being called sir as you do being called ma'am," Brodrick said with a smile, making a point to call her Savannah.

"I will try never to make that mistake again, Brodrick."

"See that you don't."

Brodrick and Savannah got on the elevator and headed down to the reception area, where Heather had assembled the people who weren't performing key functions within the company.

"Here's what's going to happen. The people are assembled outside the elevator. When the doors open, we'll step out and get this show on the road."

"Sounds good."

The doors opened. Brodrick and Savannah stepped out, and the show he orchestrated began in earnest. Brodrick made his speech. He surprised everybody because it was brief for a change. Then he introduced Savannah, and she had less to say than he did. Then, as promised, Brodrick walked Savannah around and introduced her to members of management and the members of the board of directors who were in the building at the time.

Most of them had never met Savannah, and others had questions about why, of all the qualified candidates, he chose to hire Savannah Ayers, a senior vice president for three years at BHV Power, to be the next president of Intuitive Energy. Others asked if he understood that she would be the first person of color to head an energy company.

After spending considerable time reassuring some and promising that he understood fully the implications of what he was doing, Brodrick and Savannah made their way back up to their floor and went to her office.

"Before you get too comfortable, I've put together a press conference to introduce you."

"When?"

"Today." He looked at his watch. "We'll get started around ten fifteen. I would like you to reassure investors that the stock price will rebound."

"I don't know if I'd be comfortable making such a broad statement, especially since I've only recently been appointed president and have not yet been thoroughly informed about the company's future outlook."

"This is your honeymoon period, Savannah. Just get up there and feed the press a line of bullshit about growth largely due to marketing and promoting power. Speak optimistically about Intuitive Energy's labor and the workforce. And speak forcefully about large long-term pensions and benefits for its workers. And most importantly, extremely effective management." Brodrick stood in the doorway. "You'll be fine."

"If you say so," Savannah said as she watched Brodrick walk out of her office. "It will be all right," she said aloud, mostly to reassure herself.

At the press conference, Brodrick said a few words, which once again surprised those in attendance, and then he introduced Savannah. She stepped up to the podium and turned on her power smile.

"Good morning, ladies and gentlemen. As Brodrick told you, my name is Savannah Ayers, and I am the new president here at Intuitive Energy. And I am happy to take your questions."

Hands shot up everywhere. Savannah pointed.

"I'm gonna go ahead and ask the question everybody wants an answer to. What is your plan to raise Intuitive Energy's falling stock price?"

"What I plan to do hasn't been decided because"—Savannah made a show of looking at her watch—"I've only been in the building for two hours and most of that was spent walking around meeting my new colleagues.

However, I do want to answer your very important question. The only answer I can give you today is that I plan to work with Brodrick Fowler, the chairman of the board here at Intuitive Energy. Once we have our ducks in a row, I'll be implementing a plan that prompts growth due largely to marketing and promoting power."

"Thank you."

Savannah pointed to someone. She waited until the crowd quieted down before she asked her question.

"Are you optimistic about the future of Intuitive Energy?"

"I am optimistic about Intuitive Energy's future because of our extraordinary labor and the workforce." Savannah glanced over her shoulder at Brodrick. "I've been told our extraordinary labor and the workforce are the best in the business."

That was the last of the underhand softball questions.

From that point forward, every question was one that Savannah could not answer because she hadn't been fully briefed on the financial future of the company of which she was now president.

That's why I thought this was a bad idea.

Good or bad idea, there she was, and Savannah answered each question and answered it in a way that satisfied the reporter and didn't make her look like she didn't know what she was talking about.

Most importantly, Savannah answered their questions in a way that did not, in any way, commit her to anything other than, "We'll put together a study group to research that. But let me put it to you this way. Today is my wedding day to Intuitive Energy." Savannah held her arms out. "And this is my wedding reception."

The assembled reporters laughed.

Brodrick was happy because the press loved Savannah, and that was what he needed. He had seen her do a press conference while she was at BHV Power, and he was impressed with how she handled it. Her ability to deal with the press was one of the reasons why he hired her.

"Tomorrow morning, I'll be going on my honeymoon," she all but sang, and the reporters laughed again. "After that, I am sure I'll be just brimming and bursting at the seams with the answers to specific questions. So, let's do this again in a couple of weeks, and I promise you will not be able to shut me up."

Brodrick stepped in front of the microphone. "That's all for today. Thank you all for coming." He walked away from the podium with Savannah. "Outstanding work, Savannah. You played them like an old Texas fiddle. And I get the fever every time I hear that tune," he said, referencing Merle Haggard's "Texas Fiddle Song."

"Thank you, Brodrick."

"I knew I made the right decision." He glanced at his watch as they got to their elevator. "You need to start making your way to the television station."

In addition to the press conference, Brodrick arranged for Savannah to record an interview for the next day's showing of *Good Morning Houston*.

"I need to get my purse from my office, and then I'll be on my way." The elevator came, and they stepped on. "And I spoke with my assistant at BHV. Her name is Kiera Shields."

"Let me guess, she jumped at the chance."

"Just like you said."

"We're a good company, Savannah. People want to work here."

"You're right." The elevator arrived on their floor. "Look at me. I jumped at the chance because this is a great place to work." They got off and went their separate ways. "I'll call you when I get back."

"You've got Duncan when you get back," Brodrick said as he walked down the hall to his office. "Much more important."

Duncan Anderson was the CFO of Intuitive Energy. When she returned from her celebration lunch with her girlfriends, Savannah was to be briefed on the financial health of the company.

When she got outside the building, there was a limousine waiting to take her to the station. When she arrived, she was running a bit late and was rushed to get her hair and makeup done. Once she was finished, Savannah was taken to the set to record the interview with Anisa Jimenez.

"Welcome to *Good Morning Houston,* Savannah," Anisa began.

"Thank you for having me."

"So, tell me, Savannah, how did you get to where you are today?"

"I graduated from Texas Southern University," Savannah began. "An HBCU."

"That's a historically Black college or university," Anisa clarified.

"I graduated with a bachelor of science in computer science, and I earned a master of science in energy management at the University of Texas at Dallas. After that, I went to work for serval energy and energy-related companies. But it was my position as a senior VP at BHV that propelled me into this new position."

"You are the first person of color to head an energy company. How does that happen?"

"That I'm the first? I couldn't explain that if we had all day to talk about it."

"That is so true."

She pointed to herself. "But if you're asking me, Savannah Ayers, I believe and have always believed that each of our experiences in life, our parents, our siblings, teachers, friends, everything I've done, places I've worked, and the people I've come in contact with through the years all have prepared me for this moment, right here, right now. And right here, right now, I am prepared to take on this challenge."

Savannah killed the rest of the interview.

She returned to the office in the limousine riding high, and Savannah planned to ride that high through lunch with her girls and into that afternoon's meeting about the financial health of the company.

Savannah met her girlfriends: an accountant, Thalia Blackburn, and an attorney, Ciara Reynolds. Both she'd known for years. They met for lunch at Palate Pleasures, a gourmet seafood eatery. Over a baked Dijon salmon and lobster thermidor lunch, the three friends talked about their men.

Savannah talked about her husband, Greyson, who was a driver for FedEx, and Thalia talked about her husband, Cedric Winters. Like her, he was an accountant. Ciara wasn't married, but she had been engaged to a lawyer, Zack McConnell, for the last two years, so she had a lot to say about him.

"Before we go any further . . ." Thalia raised her wine goblet. "Congratulations on your first day at the office."

"And to your continuous success," Ciara added, and they drank to that.

"Thank you. Thank you both."

"So, how does it feel to be the president of a major Texas energy company?" Ciara asked.

"Ask me in a month. Right now, it's like Brodrick says. This is my honeymoon period. I'm sure they're gonna handle me with kid gloves until I really get waist-deep in the muck and mire before I actually know what's really going on."

"True. And even then, there's gonna be things, and yes, I'm talking about financial things that the board is not going to want you to know anything about," Thalia warned. "So, protect yourself."

"That is so true. So, find ways to protect yourself," Ciara warned. "At all times and at all costs."

"I will. Believe that."

"Make sure that you do," Thalia concurred.

"I will. Like my freedom depended on it," Savannah promised.

"How's Greyson taking all this?" Thalia asked.

"Are you kidding?" Ciara asked and laughed. "They're probably running around the house butt-ass naked, fucking on every piece of furniture in the house."

"You would think, with us being 'empty nesters,'" Savannah said with air quotes. "But no. I thought with the kids gone that he would drop some of the extra shifts he'd been working." Savannah shook her head. "He's working just as much as he always has."

"I'm sorry," Ciara said.

"No sex at all?" Thalia asked.

Savannah dropped and shook her head.

The last time had been before their son, Marley, went away for college. That was almost a month ago, and nothing since then. When Greyson came home, it was always after nine. He'd eat something, take a shower, and then it was off to bed.

"I'm sorry," Ciara said. Zack may not have satisfied her every time, but at least they were having sex.

"I didn't know," Thalia said, thinking that Cedric might be a cheating asshole, but at least they were fucking. She looked at her beautiful friend, and the sad look on her face told her that she needed to change the subject. "Tell us about your new office."

"I know you must have a nice office," Ciara said.

"I do. It's a corner office with a large picture window, and the view of the city is spectacular. Brodrick and I are the only ones on that floor. My office is on one end of the hall, and he is on the other."

"If nothing else, you'll enjoy the view," Ciara said.

"I said the same thing, but I didn't know that Brodrick was standing in the doorway. He said, 'I sincerely hope you accomplish more than that while you're here.'"

"No, he didn't," Thalia laughed.

"Yes, he did."

Ciara looked at her watch. "Look at the time." She finished her wine. "I need to make my way back to the office. I have a client consultation this afternoon."

"I guess I need to get back to the office too," Savannah said. "I've got a meeting with Duncan Anderson, CFO of the company."

"That is the beauty of being your own boss. I can take as long a lunch as I want. I'm not gonna fire me," Thalia said. "You two go on and go. This is my party."

"This will be the last time. Brodrick told me that, sometime today, I'll get my American Express black card. So, from then on, these lunches are my treat."

"You sure?" Ciara asked Thalia as she got up.

"Yes, I'm sure. Go on, get outta here," Thalia said as she watched Savannah and Ciara rush off to get back to work. She signaled for their server.

"Bring me another glass of chardonnay and the check, please."

Chapter Three

Savannah returned to her office to be briefed on the financial health of Intuitive Energy by Duncan Anderson, CFO of the company. She asked Heather to let Duncan know that she was back and could meet anytime he was ready. Savannah hadn't been back in her office for a minute or two before Duncan called and said that he'd be ready to meet at three o'clock in the conference room.

"That will be fine. I'm looking forward to meeting you."

"I am as well."

At a quarter to three, Savannah got her things together and left her office to go to the conference room. When she arrived, Duncan and his team were there getting set up to do a presentation for her.

"Good afternoon, everyone," Savannah said when she came into the conference room. Duncan introduced himself to her and then introduced Savannah to his team.

"It's good to meet all of you. Shall we get to it?" she said and took her seat at the head of the conference table.

"By all means," Duncan said.

One of his teammates dimmed the lights, and they watched a twenty-minute presentation of the company and its outlook for the future. It presented a very optimistic outlook for future growth. Savannah got the sense that this was the type of presentation that they would show to potential investors and not the new president of the company.

“That was good information,” Savannah said. “I noted that Intuitive Energy has adopted a mark-to-market accounting system.”

“Yes.” Duncan paused. “Our use of mark-to-market accounting allows Intuitive to value assets and liabilities based on what they could be bought or sold for in today’s marketplace rather than their original price. It’s a valuation method that provides greater transparency about our financial position.”

“Yes,” Savannah said impatiently. “I am well aware of what mark-to-market accounting is,” she lied. Thalia had mentioned what mark-to-marking accounting was once or twice in passing.

But they don’t know that.

“However, if not supervised correctly, it can also introduce significant volatility and cause market disruptions,” Savannah remembered Thalia saying. Duncan’s team looked at each other and then at Duncan.

“There are Financial Accounting Standards Board guidelines for mark-to-market under generally accepted accounting principles,” Duncan said. Savannah nodded, and he moved on. “Alanna Cochran has been brought in as COO of Intuitive Energy Development Corporation, a unit formed to pursue international markets.”

“What will she be responsible for?”

“She’ll be responsible for making decisions for the projects, financial planning, management of financial risk, recordkeeping, and financial reporting.”

“Who does she report to?”

“Alanna is a direct report to you, Savannah.”

“Anything else that I need to be made aware of?” she asked angrily. Getting the information that she wanted to hear seemed to be like pulling teeth, and Savannah wondered why.

"Gordon Delgado has been tasked with creating forms for off-balance sheet partnerships. And there will be many off-balance sheet partnerships and transactions."

"And who does Mr. Delgado report to?"

"Gordan is also a direct report to you, Savannah."

Savannah knew enough about accounting to know that off-balance sheet financing was a practice that would not appear on Intuitive Energy's balance sheet. It was legal so long as Intuitive Energy followed accounting regulations. If, however, it was used to hide information from the public or regulators, it became illegal. That had occurred at one of the companies she'd worked at before she became vice president at BHV. Savannah was glad that one of her best friends was an accountant who really understood what all that meant.

As Duncan wrapped up his presentation, his team gathered their materials and left the conference room thinking that Savannah Ayers knew more than they were led to believe.

Savannah felt blindsided and was floored by everything he'd told her. Duncan gathered his papers and put them in his briefcase. Then he watched as the last of his staff left the conference room.

"You wanna know the truth?"

"It would be nice."

"Why do you think they gave Tia Richards a golden parachute and brought you in?" He leaned closer to Savannah. "You're the cleanup woman. You are now the face of everything that goes on here."

Savannah felt her stomach drop.

"Sorry. I thought you knew."

Duncan left the conference room and left Savannah alone with her thoughts. She laughed to herself and stood up. Savannah gathered her things and left the conference room. When Savannah got back to her office, she picked up the phone and called Kiera.

"Kiera Shields."

"Have you submitted your resignation yet?"

"Not yet. I got busy and haven't had a chance."

"Don't."

Kiera thought that Savannah was retracting the job offer, but it was anything but that.

"I need you to make the resignation effective immediately. I need you here at eight o'clock tomorrow morning, watching my back."

"I am typing it up right now," Kiera said, feeling an overwhelming sense of relief because she was so ready to get out of there. "What happened?"

"We'll talk later. I'll come by your house tonight, and I'll tell you all about it."

"See you tonight. I'll text you when I hand it to Asshole and walk out of here laughing."

"Sounds good. See you later." Savannah hung up, and then she called Thalia.

"What's up?"

"I need to talk to you about something," Savannah said. She looked at her watch. "I can be to your office in ten minutes. I know you must get home to feed your kids."

"Meet me here, and then you can come back with me to the house if I have to go."

"See you in ten minutes."

Savannah gathered her things and was about to leave to go to Thalia's office when her phone rang. "Savannah Ayers," she said.

"Can you come to my office, Savannah?" Brodrick asked.

"Be there in a minute," Savannah said and put her purse back in the drawer. Then she went to see what Brodrick wanted to talk about.

"You wanted to see me?" Savannah said when she walked into his office.

"Come in and have a seat, Savannah," Brodrick said. "How did it go with Duncan?"

Rather than tell him that Duncan's presentation raised several red flags for her, Savannah said, "It was a good presentation."

"Did you have any questions or concerns?"

"If I do, I'm sure as I become more familiar with the way things are done here, I'll find my answers. If not, I know I can always come and talk to you about any questions or concerns I have."

Brodrick nodded. "I wanted to make you aware that Lauren Beard will be establishing numerous limited liability special-purpose entities." He tapped her personally because Beard was well acquainted with the burgeoning deregulated energy markets he wanted to exploit.

"For what purpose?"

"The purpose is to help make Intuitive Energy the biggest wholesaler of gas and electricity. I conservatively estimate that will allow us to trade over twenty billion per quarter."

Brodrick knew that the limited liability special-purpose entities would allow Intuitive Energy to transfer some of its liabilities off its books. That would allow Intuitive Energy to maintain its stock price and keep its critical investment-grade credit ratings.

But Savannah doesn't need to know that, he thought but didn't mention to her.

"Anything else?"

"I don't believe it was a part of Duncan's presentation, but I've committed us to repay Clearwater Capital Partners' investment with interest."

Brodrick wanted to be able to show a profit on the books. He understood that debts and losses put into offshore entities would not be included in the company's financial statements.

But Savannah doesn't need to know that either.

"No, Brodrick. That wasn't part of Duncan's presentation," Savannah said, and that sinking feeling in her stomach returned. Duncan's words, "You are now the face of everything that goes on here," took on a fresh meaning.

"Understandable." Brodrick didn't say anything for a few seconds. He looked Savannah in the eyes. "This is one of those times when you and I have to be in perfect tune. Walking the same walk, talking the same talk."

"I understand, and I agree. There are certain things that Duncan is not privy to, that only need to be known at this level," Savannah said, and Brodrick nodded.

"You understand." Brodrick smiled. "Any observations about your first day?"

"I'm glad it's over," Savannah said and paused to look at Brodrick for his reaction. "Tomorrow I can start doing the work of running this company with your help."

"I know it's getting late, and I got the feeling that you were leaving when I called."

"I was."

"Go on. Get out of here, and I'll see you at eight o'clock tomorrow morning."

"For coffee, snack cakes, and sweets of every variety known to man."

"See you in the morning, Savannah."

"Good night, Brodrick."

Once Savannah was out of the building and on her way to her car, she called Thalia.

"I thought you'd be here by now."

"I would have been, but Brodrick stopped me on the way and wanted to make me aware of some things. I can be there in ten minutes."

"Come on."

When Savannah arrived at the offices of Levanter Auditoria, she spoke to everybody and headed straight to Thalia's office. She ran into Cedric on the way.

"Hey, Savannah."

"How are you, Cedric?"

"Doing great. Congratulations on being named president of Intuitive Energy."

"Thank you."

"Thalia is in her office. Come on. I'll be your escort."

"You do know that, after all these years, I do know the way to your wife's office."

"I do," Cedric said and continued to walk alongside Savannah. Thalia looked up when they came into her office. "Look who I found wandering the halls."

"Hey, Savannah." Thalia looked at Cedric. "I was expecting her."

"Savannah, as always," Cedric said to her as he started to leave Thalia's office, "it was great seeing you, and like I said, congratulations. President at Intuitive Energy. That's quite the accomplishment."

"Thank you, Cedric." Savannah sat down in one of the chairs in front of Thalia's desk.

"You done for the day?" Thalia asked Cedric.

"Yeah. I'll see you when you get home."

"Start dinner for the children," Thalia said as Cedric walked out of her office. "So, what's up with you? Did they pop your balloon this afternoon when you got briefed on the financial future of Intuitive Energy?"

Savannah shook and then dropped her head. "Yes. I was glad I remembered the few things you mentioned, like mark-to-market accounting, or I would have been sitting there like Willie Lump-Lump not knowing what they were talking about. They showed me a presentation, which I believe is for potential investors, and they thought I didn't know anything about accounting."

Savannah laughed. “Which I don’t. You’re my accounting knowledge.”

From there, Savannah told Thalia about the things that Duncan and Brodrick told her, from the mark-to-market accounting system to the off-balance sheet partnerships, to limited liability special-purpose entities and Brodrick’s promise to repay an investment with interest to show a profit on its books.

“All that does seem, on its face, a little off the path. But everything you told me about is perfectly legal. Accounting Standards Board mark-to-market accounting is a generally accepted accounting principle. And you can’t argue with their success. But I would keep my eyes open and make friends with somebody to watch my back.”

“I have Kiera Shields, my old assistant at BHV, coming in tomorrow morning at eight o’clock.”

“Good for you,” Thalia said and got her purse out of the drawer. “I would make Ciara aware of what you told me.” Savannah stood up, and they walked out together. “But like I said, everything that they’re doing is perfectly legal. Do you think you’re overreacting?”

“I don’t know.” But Savannah didn’t think she was. “Maybe I am.”

“You are now the face of everything that goes on here.”

It was almost seven o’clock when Savannah arrived at Kiera’s house. When she opened the door to let Savannah in, she was wearing sweats and a tank top. It caught Savannah off guard because Kiera was always dressed in the latest fashions.

“What?”

“Nothing.” Savannah giggled. “I’ve just never seen you so . . . so casual.”

"What did you think, I walk around the house in Monique Lhuillier dresses and Jimmy Choo slingback pumps?"

"Yeah, well, kinda."

Kiera laughed. "Can I get you something to drink?"

"No. I'm good."

"So, tell me, what is going on at Intuitive Energy that I quit my job for?"

"How'd that go?"

"Great, from my point of view," Kiera said, and she began to get excited about what she was about to tell Savannah. "I had just come from the printer with my resignation when Asshole screamed, 'Kiera, my office now!'"

"Oh, no," Savannah said because the Kiera she knew didn't take shit from any man.

Ever.

"So, I go into his office, and I say, 'You wanted to see me?' He yells so loud it gets the attention of everybody in the unit, 'Yeah, I wanted to know if you're dumb or just plain stupid.'"

"Oops."

"Oops is right."

Savannah was smiling because she knew what was going to happen in that office.

"I yell right back at him, 'You know what, I was gonna wait until the end of the day to give this to you.' I threw the letter of resignation on his desk, and I yelled, 'I resign effective immediately.' I went and made a show of packing up my stuff. Asshole came out, and he apologized and asked me to stay until he could get somebody in to replace me."

"What did you say?"

"I got in his face, and I yelled, 'Hell no, you fucking asshole!' I picked up my stuff and walked out of there to a standing ovation."

"No, you didn't," Savannah laughed.

"Yes. Elsie, Aleena, Bailey, and Carrie stood up and gave me a standing ovation. Carrie said, 'I'm right behind you, girl.'"

"They will fire him if the whole department quits on him."

"He needs to be ready for that because it's coming. Now, tell me, what's going on over there?"

"Thalia says I'm overreacting, but throughout the day, I had a feeling that what they're doing isn't quite right."

"But Thalia thinks you're overreacting."

"She said that everything they're doing may be unorthodox, but according to the Accounting Standards Board, mark-to-market accounting is a generally accepted accounting principle. But I'd feel better with you there watching my back."

"I'm there. Now, let's talk about my salary."

Chapter Four

When attorney Ciara Reynolds met Zack McConnell, he said that it was love at first sight.

"I plan to make you my wife one day," he told her on their first date.

Ciara smiled, but she had heard that type of talk from many men before Zack came along.

"We'll see how that works out for you," she said that day.

However, Zack McConnell was a great catch. He was a fellow attorney with a white-shoe firm, Hayes, Bowers & Farley, and he was on the fast track to make partner. And he was gorgeous. He was a tall, dark, extremely handsome dark-skinned man, and had a muscular, chiseled body, a goatee, and the cutest dimples Ciara had ever seen.

Over the next six months, Zack wined and dined Ciara, showered her with expensive gifts, and took her on trips to exotic destinations.

Six months later, he proposed marriage and gave her a fourteen-karat white gold 4.5-carat lab-grown diamond engagement ring that he paid $14,000 for. Zack took Ciara to dinner at Bistecca Italia, an Italian steak house. He hired a violin quartet, and he got down on one knee over veal tartare.

"Ciara Reynolds, will you marry me?"

"Yes. Yes, of course, I'll marry you."

That was two years ago, and in that time, Zack had not committed to a date for them to be married. He had several excuses as to why he couldn't commit. His favorite seemed to be career changes or some big case that would lead to advancement at the firm if he just committed more time and put in more effort. To Ciara, his selfishness and indecision were the reasons he wouldn't set a date.

"Why should he when he's got me on lock and he's getting all of his needs met? He gets all the sex he wants, and I do everything he needs or could possibly want," Ciara complained to Thalia. "At this point, Zack doesn't see any reason to change anything because I give him everything he wants."

"Maybe you don't need to be so much on lock and stop giving him everything he wants," was the advice Thalia offered her. Ciara received pretty much the same advice from Savannah.

"Girl, throw that one back. There are other fish in the sea who would fall all over themselves to be with a woman like you."

It was true.

Ciara Reynolds was a beautiful woman with a successful law practice. Although it wasn't a white-shoe firm like Hayes, Bowers & Farley, she, too, was on the partner track at Lawson, Logan, and Associates.

Even though Ciara was engaged to Zack, men were falling all over themselves trying to get with her. She might go out with some of her suitors, have dinner, see a show, or meet up for cocktails after doing battle in court. But at the end of the night, Ciara would tell each one that she was engaged to a wonderful man.

"Who I don't cheat on."

Then she would call Zack to see if he was available, and if he wasn't working another late night or in a client meeting over dinner, she'd go see him, and they'd have sex.

Ciara would be the first one to admit to herself, but not to anybody else, especially to Savannah and Thalia, that she'd had better lovers, but he satisfied her, and when he didn't, she had something for that.

On that particular evening, Zack and Ciara went to the theater, where they had orchestra seats to see a play produced by some friends of hers. *No Tears in the End* was about a once-popular author who had fallen on hard times both personally and professionally but felt that he had authored the best book of his career.

After leaving the play, they had a late dinner at the Thai Front, which was one of Ciara's favorite restaurants. She always ordered the pad kra pao moo, which was stir-fried Thai basil and pork. However, that night, she ordered tom yum goong, which was hot and sour shrimp soup.

"Why the change?" Zack asked.

"Some people have been encouraging me to try new things."

"I'll have the pad Thai stir-fried noodles with shrimp." He handed the server the menu and picked up his drink. Zack took a sip. "Savannah and Thalia, are they the ones doing this encouraging?"

"Yes. How did you guess?"

"Who else would it be?" he asked and seemed to be waiting for an answer. When she said nothing, he pressed on with his point. "I know you don't agree with me on this, but I think they have entirely too much influence over you. They can tell you something, and suddenly, it is the law set in stone."

"You are absolutely right. I don't agree with you. This may come as some surprise to you, but I can and often do think for myself at times. I don't need you or, frankly, them to do my thinking for me."

"Don't get upset. I'm just making conversation. Expressing my opinion."

"I think that since you've expressed that opinion more times than I care to count and it always falls on deaf ears, maybe you'd be better served to let that go."

"Maybe I should."

After what turned out to be a contentious meal, Ciara and Zack went to her house and had what she considered to be uninspired sex, and he fell fast asleep. On nights like that, Ciara had gotten in the habit of breaking out Ava Vibrator Wand to do what Zack, at times, couldn't accomplish.

Bring her to orgasm.

Fortunately for Ciara, once Zack got his and fell asleep, he could sleep through a hurricane, so she could lie in bed next to him, get hers, put Ava back in her nightstand, and go to sleep.

When she woke up in the morning, Zack was gone. He left Ciara a note that said he went to the gym to get in a workout before he met with Cloud Harbor, which, as the name implied, was a cloud storage company.

"Whatever," Ciara said as she got out of bed.

She headed for the bathroom to shower and get ready for work. She had client meetings that morning as well. She selected a light blue Boss V-neck business dress and headed for the office.

The client was a startup cybersecurity provider called Digital Forge. During the meeting, Ciara advised them on intellectual property protection, IP ownership, their business structure and formation, shareholder agreements, funding agreements, and employment law.

Ciara's afternoon client meeting was with Tobias and Leona Chandler. They were the owners of Oil and Gas Production Equipment Inc., a Houston-based business that was started by Leona's father, Solomon McKnight.

They sold land rigs, offshore rigs, drilling equipment, tubular equipment, electrical equipment, pressure control equipment, and support equipment to the oil companies.

When Tobias Chandler began working there as an account executive, Leona took an interest in him, and it wasn't long before they were married. Shortly after, Leona forced her father out of the business that he started, and Tobias became CEO of Oil and Gas Production Equipment Inc.

As it turned out, it may have seemed cruel, but Leona had done the right thing for all parties concerned. Under Tobias Chandler's leadership, the company quadrupled its business. The Chandlers made a fortune. Nowadays, the couple was living on the island of Saint Barts in a fifteen-bedroom mansion on the beach.

This would be the first time that Ciara met with the Chandlers. They had been Sharon Mason's clients; however, she decided that the travel the account demanded had put a strain on her marriage.

Once they were shown into her office, Ciara stood up to greet them. Leona's face lit up at the sight of her in that light blue V-neck dress. Tobias's reaction was similar to that of his wife's. Ciara was a bit surprised because Tobias was so much older than Leona. To her, he looked as if he was in his late forties or early fifties, as opposed to Leona, who was, at best, in her early thirties.

"Please come in and have a seat," Ciara said. "I am Ciara Reynolds, and I am now officially your attorney of record."

"Leona Chandler, and this is my husband, Tobias," she said and shook hands with Ciara while looking directly into her eyes. Leona held her hand and continued looking directly into Ciara's eyes.

"It's a pleasure to meet you both."

"I have to tell you, Ciara, you are absolutely stunning," Leona said.

"Thank you for the compliment."

Ciara looked at Leona and admired her tanned skin. She was wearing a white sleeveless Brandon Maxwell V-neck slip dress that showed off her abundant cleavage. *And she is wearing it well,* Ciara thought and continued. "This is just an informal meeting so I can have an opportunity to learn what you do and how I can be of service to you."

At that point, Tobias went into a long explanation of what their company sold. Leona looked bored during his explanation. It seemed as if she was content to look into Ciara's eyes while he talked.

"I'd need to review those records," Ciara said.

That's when Leona spoke up. "We don't travel with our records. If you want to review them, you'll have to come to Saint Barts and stay a couple of days with us. Is that going to be an issue for you?"

"Not at all. When Sharon turned over the account, she mentioned that some travel was required."

"You're not married, are you?" Leona asked.

"No."

"Sharon informed us that the travel requirements were putting a strain on her marriage. So you can surely understand that we would like to avoid that happening to us again."

"I understand," Ciara said and thought about telling them that she was engaged, but since Zack hadn't set a date, she was still a single woman.

After work, Ciara went to the gym to get her daily workout in. When she was finished, she called Zack.

"You've reached the voicemail box of Zack McConnell, attorney at law. Please leave a detailed message and your number. I will return your call as soon as possible."

"This is Ciara Reynolds, attorney at law. How did it go with Cloud Harbor? I wanted to see if you wanted to grab a meal or whatever. Call me when you get a minute. Bye-bye. Love you."

That was the message she left.

"Now what?"

It was still early, and Ciara was hungry because she hadn't taken the time to eat that day. She didn't feel like eating alone, so she called a man she met a couple of weeks ago. His name was Rahim Dalton, and they'd been exchanging text messages. At the end of each exchange, Rahim always included an invitation to have dinner or drinks with him. Each time, she made up some excuse as to why she wasn't available for dinner or drinks. Ciara sent him a text.

Busy?

Rahim replied immediately. No. I was just thinking about you. I'm not doing anything. What's up?

I wanted to know if you were free for dinner tonight.

Ciara's phone rang immediately.

"Yes. I am free for dinner tonight." Rahim paused. "You are talking about having dinner with you, right?"

"Yes, Rahim. I'm talking about you and I getting together and sharing a meal," she said, and she got a text message from Zack.

Still at the office. Meeting with senior management. Sorry, I can't do dinner tonight. But call me later tonight and we'll get together then.

Ciara rolled her eyes. *Not tonight.*

"Have you ever been to a place called Aegean Bites?" she asked.

"The Greek restaurant. I've been there before. The food is good there."

"Why don't you meet me there in, say, an hour?"

"Looking forward to seeing you again."

"I am too," Ciara said, unlocked her Audi A6, and went to meet Rahim.

Over pastitsio, souvlaki, and Fisher Vineyards cabernet sauvignon, Rahim told Ciara about his job as an architectural and engineering manager. She talked about the law. They had a good time. The conversation was engaging, and as Rahim said, the food was good there.

At the end of the evening, Rahim walked Ciara to her car.

"I had a good time tonight."

"So did I."

"We should do it again sometime."

Ciara unlocked the car. "We should."

"Something else to look forward to." Rahim paused. "But, you know, I got the impression that I was just the fill-in dinner date for the man you really wanted to have dinner with."

"Am I that obvious?"

"No, not really. It's just the impression I got. I could be wrong. I hope I am because I really do wanna see you again, Ciara."

"Call me."

Ciara opened the car door and got in. She started the car and rolled down the window. He leaned against the door.

"I will." He stood up and stepped back from the car. "Good night, Ciara."

"Good night, Rahim. We'll talk soon," she said and put the Audi in drive and left Rahim standing and waving.

Ciara drove home thinking that she had a good time with Rahim and that if she weren't engaged to Zack, she might go out with him again.

"Second dates are a slippery slope," Ciara said aloud as she drove. "So, no. I won't be taking your calls or replying to your texts anymore. Sorry, Rahim."

When Ciara arrived at her house, she called Zack to see if he was finished with senior management and wanted to come over. Dinner with sexy Rahim had her feeling some kind of way. It was late, so assuming he'd be finished, Ciara called.

"You've reached the voicemail box of Zack McConnell, attorney at law. Please leave a detailed message and your number. I will return your call as soon as possible."

"I called."

That was the message she left for him, and then she called him right back.

"You asked me to call you later tonight so we can get together. I gotta say, this shit is getting old."

Ciara slammed her cell phone on the couch next to her and cursed the ground Zack walked on and went to her bedroom. As she got undressed and got in the shower, she thought about the advice that she received from Thalia and Savannah. "Maybe you don't need to be so much on lock," and "Stop giving him everything he wants," and "Throw that one back."

"Savannah's right," she said aloud as she ran the loofah over her skin. "There are other fish in the sea. And maybe it's time I find one who actually has time for me."

Chapter Five

Thalia Blackburn went home after work after her brief but troubling meeting with Savannah. Although she suggested that she may have been overreacting, some of the things that she mentioned were more than unorthodox and might be legal, according to the Accounting Standards Board, but they were often used for purposes other than transparency.

That was why she also recommended that, in addition to bringing in her old assistant from BHV to watch her back, she talk to Ciara about everything going on at Intuitive Energy. *Savannah being the first person of color to head an energy company may be for reasons other than her qualifications.* Thalia had been an accountant a long time, and she'd seen and heard of companies on their last leg bring in somebody to land the plane or take the fall for it all. And she'd been black a lot longer, so Thalia knew that Savannah wouldn't be the first fall guy of color.

Thalia Winters started Winters Accounting Services while she was in college doing the books for local companies. After graduation, her company grew. She met Cedric Blackburn at an accounting convention, and she fell in love. They were married, and they merged their companies to form Levanter Auditoria. They had three children. Aliza was 12, Eric was 10, and the youngest, Sylvie, was 9.

When she got home, the children were there, but Thalia noted that despite Cedric saying that he was on his way home, he wasn't there. His car wasn't in the garage.

Aliza and Sylvie were in the living room watching something on Disney+. Eric was in his room playing video games, as usual.

"Hi, Mom," the girls said when she came into the house.

"How are my two favorite girls?"

"Shhh," they both said.

"Don't shhh me. I'm your mother. Where's your father?" she asked, even though she knew he wasn't there. There was the possibility that he had been there and just ran to the store and would be back.

"I don't know," Aliza said without turning away from the television. "He hasn't been here."

Knowing how annoying it is when somebody talks to you when you're trying to watch television, Thalia left her daughters alone and went into the kitchen to start cooking dinner.

After the children were fed and Cedric was still not home, Thalia called him, but she got no answer. She was about to send a text when he called her back.

"Sorry I missed your call. What's up?"

"I thought you were coming home."

"I was. But Frankie Poole with Shopzed called."

"He's the online reseller you've been pursuing, right?"

"That's right. You do pay attention when I tell you things."

She laughed. "It's you who doesn't pay me any attention when I tell you things."

"Untrue."

It was obvious to Thalia that he had covered the phone with his hand. "The food just came, so I'll call you back later."

"You don't need to call. You just need to come home and take care of your wife. What time do you think you'll be finished?" Thalia glanced at the clock on the stove. It was seven forty-five.

"Like I said, food just came. I'm thinking half an hour for dinner and conversation. I told you how talkative Frankie Poole can be once he gets going. Another forty minutes for cocktails and more conversation. I'm thinking ten, ten thirty at the very latest."

"See you then," she said, and hung up without waiting for him to comment. "More like tell me another lie, you mean." Thalia thought about camping out in the living room until he walked through the door. "But what would be the point? You know he's not gonna be home at no ten, ten thirty."

She got up from the table in the kitchen. After she cleaned up the kitchen and washed the dishes, she went into the living room and sat on the couch to watch TV. She thought about calling Savannah to complain about what she was sure was her cheating husband. She picked up the phone and put it down immediately. Savannah had been telling her for years that Cedric had been cheating on her for years.

"And I'm not trying to hear that lecture tonight."

At ten o'clock, she turned off the television and went upstairs to their room. By ten forty-five, she was showered and ready for bed. Thalia put on her Fleur du Mal floral lace gown and waited for Cedric to come home.

It was eleven forty-five when Thalia heard the alarm beep once. It let her know that Cedric was home. He came into their bedroom and went straight into the bathroom. The next sound Thalia heard was water running. After his usual quick wash, he came out of the bathroom naked and got in bed with Thalia.

"You asleep?"

"I was, but I'm not anymore," she said with her heart beating with anticipation.

Cedric may have been a cheater, but Thalia loved to have sex. And sex with Cedric was always so magnificent. She reached around, and Cedric's soldier was standing at attention for her. She took his length in her hand and stroked it gently before she turned toward him. Thalia licked and sucked his nipple until it grew hard in her mouth.

Thalia was always hungry for Cedric, and she wanted him deep inside her. He touched her face with both hands and pulled her closer so he could kiss her. It wasn't long before their long, frenzied kiss slowed and turned tender, and each felt the absolute bliss of their tongues dancing in the other's mouth.

Cedric ran his finger down her moist lips, and he could see how drenched Thalia was from the exchange. He slid his hand along her mound, and his finger found its way to her clit. He spun Thalia around, grabbed her by her hips, and entered her in one hard thrust.

Thalia squirmed as she took in every inch of Cedric's thickness inside her warmth. Once she had taken all of him inside her, Cedric let go of her hips, and she pushed her ass against him because she wanted to feel every delicious inch.

She pushed her body into his, and Cedric grabbed her by the shoulders. He began to hit it as hard as he could. Cedric let go of her shoulders and squeezed her breast with one hand, and he reached between her legs with the other hand and fingered her clit. Cedric slowed his pace and began to long-stroke Thalia. He would pull almost completely out of her and then slowly ease his entire length back inside of her. However, Thalia wanted it hard. She threw her body into him so hard that his dick came out.

"Please, put it back in," Thalia begged.

Cedric flipped Thalia on her back and entered her so hard that it made her walls clench and release around him as he moved in and out of her.

Even if he was a cheater, Cedric filled every inch of her, and it always made her want more. As much as she could get. When he made love to her, Thalia felt like he was hers, and no other woman could know the feeling she was feeling. But she knew that wasn't true.

When Thalia worked her hips and inner muscles while licking his nipples, his body began to tremble. Thalia rocked her hips furiously into him until Cedric's entire body went rigid, and he exploded inside her.

Cheater or not, Thalia loved to have sex. And sex with Cedric was always so mind-blowing.

A hundred times a day, she thought about leaving him. However, there were more reasons than just his amazing sex that she stayed for. First and foremost, there were the children. He loved his children, and he was a great father to them. She didn't want to break up that relationship. Then, they were partners in Levanter Auditoria. How to divide their business after all these years would be a nightmare. There was also the fact that it was predominantly her high-priced clientele who were carrying the business.

Any division of the business would, more likely than not, mean her income would be greater than his. She knew in any divorce action, Cedric would fight her for custody. Aside from that getting ugly, if he were awarded custody and she got visitation, Thalia would have to pay him child support. That made Cedric cheaper to keep than throw away because he was and had been a cheater.

Chapter Six

After receiving that blow about Intuitive Energy's financial situation, Savannah went home. When she opened the garage, she was surprised to see Greyson's car. It was just after eight, and he usually got home sometime after nine. Savannah went inside thinking that more late nights were going to become the norm for her. In any case, she was glad that he was home.

"Greyson," Savannah said when she came into the house.

"In the living room."

Savannah went into the living room and found Greyson sitting on the couch. "You're home early tonight," she said, walking to the bar in the living room. "Can I get you something?"

"No, thank you."

"You don't mind if I do?"

"Not at all. How was your first day?"

"Interesting. That's what I'll call it, interesting."

"How so?"

"Their choice of accounting methods is troubling to me. But Thalia says they are perfectly legal, and I may be overreacting."

"What does your gut tell you?"

"To keep my eyes open." Savannah sat down next to Greyson. "What about you? How was your day?"

Greyson sat up a little straighter and took a deep breath. "There's no easy way to say this."

"Say what?"

"That I want a divorce."

"What?"

"I want a divorce," Greyson repeated, and Savannah could hardly believe what she was hearing.

"Why? I thought we were happy."

"You were happy, Savannah. You have and always get everything you want. But what about me? What do I have?"

"You have a wife who still loves you after all these years together. You have the home we built together and two wonderful children."

"The children are gone. And the house is yours."

"The house is ours."

"You pay the mortgage. My name is just on the deed."

"Where is this coming from? Is there somebody else?"

"No, Savannah. There's nobody else. This is about you and me."

"What is it then?"

"I have always felt out of place when we would go to the many parties and events a woman in your position gets invited to. And now it will only get worse. I can hear it now. 'I'm president of Intuitive Energy.' 'And what does your husband do?' 'He's a driver for FedEx.'"

"You could have gone back to school, graduated, and gotten a better job."

"When? After you graduated, you couldn't find a job that would support us with two kids. I had to keep working, and you went to grad school."

"After grad school, I asked you if you wanted to go back to finish college, but you weren't interested."

"The long and short of it is . . ." Greyson began because Savannah all but begged him to go back and finish college, but he wasn't interested. "I've always felt emasculated by your success."

"I think that we should try going to counseling before we take this step."

"What is counseling gonna do for us at this point, Savannah? Is it going to turn back the hands of time for me to go back and finish college? No, it can't do that. Is counseling going to make me feel like any more of a man? No. It's not. I gave that up years ago. I'll never get that back."

"Why can't we try?"

"Honestly, Savannah, we are too far gone for that to help."

"Don't do this to us, to me, not today. Today, of all days when I need you to be there with and for me, this is what you decide to do?"

"I think it's for the best if I stay in a hotel until we work things out."

"What's to work out?" Savannah started to cry. "You just told me that there's nothing we can do to save our marriage. So what's to work out?"

"Nothing." Greyson stood up. "I'll come get my things soon."

"Whatever," Savannah said through her tears.

"Goodbye, Savannah. I'm sorry it came to this."

"Whatever," Savannah said, and she watched Greyson walk out of the house along with her marriage.

Savannah finished another drink and sat on the couch for a while before she got up and ran a hot bath. She got in the tub with a glass of wine and reflected on the marriage that had come to an end.

Savannah Townson met Greyson Ayers freshman year when they were in college. Savannah had her first child, a girl they named Alyssa, during her freshmen year at 18. She married Greyson when they were both 19, and she had her second child, a boy, Marley, when she was 20. Greyson dropped out of school that next year and got a job as a driver for FedEx to support his family while Savannah continued her education. She graduated with a degree in computer science and went on to get her master's in energy management.

Savannah got out of the tub, dried herself, and poured another glass of wine. Then she went into her bedroom and got in bed. Once she finished the wine, Savannah turned off the lights and cried herself to sleep.

The following morning, Savannah was up at six. It was going to be Kiera's first day, and as badly as she wanted to stay in bed and feel sorry for herself because her twenty-year marriage had ended, she needed to go to work.

At seven forty-five, Savannah was sitting in the reception area when Kiera got off the elevator.

"Good morning, Savannah," she said excitedly.

"Morning. Come on, I'll show you to our office." Savannah stopped. "Heather. Good morning."

"Good morning, Savannah."

"This is Kiera Shields. She's starting work today as my assistant."

"Nice to meet you, Kiera."

"Good to meet you too, Heather."

"Now, come on, I'll show you to our office. I have a meeting starting in ten minutes."

"Savannah," Heather said.

"Yes, Heather?"

"Brodrick called and said he is running late this morning, and he'll call you when he gets in his office."

"Well, then, I guess I don't have a meeting starting in ten minutes."

"Show me our office anyway," Kiera said, and they walked away from the reception area around to the elevator to Savannah and Brodrick's floor.

"Well, what do you think?" Savannah asked Kiera when they got to the office.

"I like this, Savannah. The view of the city is amazing."

"If nothing else, I'll enjoy the view from here."

"And I said, 'I sincerely hope you accomplish more than that while you're here.'"

"Good morning, Brodrick," Savannah said. "This is my assistant, Kiera Shields."

"Nice to meet you, Kiera," Brodrick said.

"Mr. Fowler is the chairman of the board at Intuitive Energy."

"And it's Brodrick. Are you ready, Savannah?"

"Let me get my tablet."

"I promise not to keep her long," Brodrick said.

Once Savannah got her tablet, she followed Brodrick to his office for coffee and pastry.

"Is there any particular way I should be answering the phone?" Kiera asked as she took a seat in her new office.

"'Intuitive Energy, Savannah Ayers's office. This is Kiera Shields. How can I help you?'" Brodrick said, walking away.

The view wasn't as magnificent as Savannah's view of the city, "But," she said, "it ain't bad."

After her morning meeting with Brodrick, Savannah returned to her office. Kiera was in her office, and when she saw Savannah coming, she gathered the messages Savannah had received in the thirty minutes she'd been gone.

"How are you settling in?"

"Great." Kiera handed Savannah the messages.

"What are these?"

"Your messages."

Savannah counted them. "There are nine messages here."

"All of them in the thirty minutes you've been gone."

"Wow. Come on in and let's get to work."

Kiera picked up her tablet and followed Savannah into the office, and they got to work returning calls. Everybody wanted something from the new president. Some were held-over requests that simply needed the approval of the president, and Tia Richards had been gone for two months.

"I'll look into that. See what needs to be done and get back to you."

Others, Savannah felt, and Kiera agreed, were departments that just wanted to see what she would say in response to certain questions. Fortunately for Savannah, she'd always been a working manager, so she knew what she was talking about. Once she let them know that she wasn't going to be fooled by foolishness, those people got pretty much the same response.

"I'll look into that. And if it is in any way feasible, I'll get back to you."

Once Savannah had returned all the messages, she and Kiera talked about what needed to be done or not done.

"And there are some things I want to ask Brodrick about."

Kiera stood up. "I'll get on it."

Savannah got to work; however, she was distracted by thoughts of the argument the night before with Greyson. His words played over and over in her mind.

"The long and short of it is that I've always felt emasculated by your success."

It was not her intention to make him feel like he was less than a man. Societal norms said that men had to be dominant. Savannah thought she had allowed Greyson to be the man of the house, despite her always making more money. She had no idea that Greyson felt inadequate and emasculated because he never breathed a word of it.

Savannah's thoughts were interrupted by Kiera.

"Savannah."

"Yes, Kiera."

"You have a call from a Hallie Gentry holding on line two. She says she's your neighbor."

"I got her. Thanks, Kiera." Savannah took the call on line two. "Good morning, Mrs. Gentry."

"Good morning, Savannah. I am so sorry to be calling you at work, but I thought you should know that there is a moving truck at your house, and men are taking things out."

"It's okay, Mrs. Gentry. I was expecting them." *Just not that quick.* "But I appreciate you calling to let me know."

"I needed to make sure. I was at the last neighborhood watch meeting, and strange trucks taking things out of houses was one of the things they said criminals do."

"Well, that is not the case here, Mrs. Gentry. Thank you very much for calling, but I have to get back to work."

It let her know that Greyson had been planning to move out for who knew how long. Savannah had no delusions about being served with divorce papers by the end of the week, if not sooner.

She needed to call Ciara. Savannah knew that she didn't do divorce cases, but she was sure that she would be able to refer her to somebody. Savannah was reaching for her cell phone when it rang. It was Thalia, who was calling to complain about Cedric.

"You got a minute?" And without waiting for an answer, she jumped right into what happened the night before. "You heard him say he was going home," she began.

Savannah let her talk for a minute or two.

"I hate to cut you off, but I need to talk to you and Ciara. Can you meet me at Boca Way Cuisine in, say"—Savannah glanced at her watch—"an hour and a half?"

"I most certainly can. What's up?"

"I'll tell you when I see you. But I gotta go. Call Ciara for me and see if she can make it."

"I can do that. No preview, huh?"

"Gotta go, Thalia. Bye," Savannah said before she could say anything else.

When Savannah arrived at the restaurant, Ciara and Thalia were there. They were on their third Aperol spritz, had crushed an order of Mexican street corn flatbread pizza, and declared Cedric the worst asshole of the month. And Ciara had convinced Thalia to set up an account on a dating app.

"What's good for the goose. You know what I'm saying?"

Savannah sat down at the table, and a waitress came to take her drink order. "I'll have whatever they're having," she said, and the waitress left the table. "I have something to tell you."

"What's that?" Thalia said and sipped her drink.

"Greyson moved out of the house last night."

"What?" Ciara said in complete shock. She thought they had the ideal marriage. One that she hoped to have one day with Zack.

"Last night, when I got home from my first big day in my new position, he told me that he had always felt emasculated by my success."

"What about going to counseling before you guys take that step?"

"I asked him that, and he said that counseling wouldn't do anything for us at this point. It couldn't give him a better job or make him feel any more like a man."

"I am so sorry, Savannah," Ciara said.

"I am too."

"I wanna change my vote on the worst asshole of the month from Cedric to Greyson."

"I second that," Thalia said as their waitress returned with Savannah's Aperol spritz.

Once the waitress was gone, Savannah made it unanimous. She raised her glass. "I declare Greyson Ayers is the worst asshole of the month. Of the fucking year." She turned to Ciara. "I need a lawyer."

"You know I don't do divorce law, but I will refer you to Summer Fitzpatrick, the best divorce lawyer in Houston."

As Savannah expected, she received the divorce papers the next night, delivered via courier when she got home. Savannah made an appointment to see Summer Fitzpatrick on Friday afternoon. Summer was the best because she hated men. That was entirely due to the way her husband and his lawyer did her during their divorce. Therefore, Summer was taking her revenge on all other men.

"All that isn't necessary in this case. I'll sign whatever and give him whatever he wants. I just want to be done with this and move on."

"Okay. I'll look over the papers, and I'll let you know if I see any red flags."

There were no red flags. Greyson didn't ask for anything. Savannah made an appointment for later in the week to sign the papers.

A court date was put on the calendar.

Chapter Seven

It was getting late in the day, and seeing that she had finished all her appointments, Ciara sent a text message to Zack. She didn't like the way their last interaction went, and to her surprise, he called her right back.

"Wow. I'm surprised you called."

"I didn't like the way we left it, and I want to try to fix things between us," Zack said.

"I was thinking the same thing."

"Surprisingly enough, I'm at home. Why don't you come on over? We can talk about it over dinner. How does that sound to you?"

"Perfect. I'm about to wrap up here."

"I'll see you soon," Zack said, pausing as his doorbell rang. "Send me a text when you're on your way."

"We'll do," Ciara said and happily ended the call.

The doorbell rang again. He went to the door to see who it was. He was surprised to see Abraham Kramer, another lawyer at Hayes, Bowers & Farley, at the door.

"Got a few minutes to . . . talk?" Abraham asked with a smile.

Zack looked at his watch. "Come on." He let him into the house. "Just talk, right?"

"Right. If that's all you wanna do."

Ciara wrapped up the research she was doing, and with that out of the way for the time being, she left her office and went to Zack's house.

It was getting late in the afternoon, so not only was she surprised that Zack was home but also that the BMW belonging to Abraham Kramer, another lawyer at Hayes, Bowers & Farley, was parked in the driveway. Since she had a key, Ciara let herself in the house and called out for him.

"Zack! Are you here?"

And that was when she heard it. Ciara followed the sound to the bedroom. There, she found Zack fucking Abraham Kramer.

"Oh, my God!" Ciara shouted and ran out of the room.

"I can explain," Zack said, running behind her to the door.

Ciara opened the door, but Zack closed it and held his hand against it.

"Let me out of here, Zack."

"I can explain."

"What's to explain?" Ciara asked, trying but not succeeding at not looking at his hard dick with an erection harder than he ever got to make love to her. "All this time, I thought you had commitment issues." She started to cry. "But the real reason is that you're gay."

"It's not what you think."

"You got shit on your dick." Her tears were streaming down her cheeks. "Now, please, if you ever felt anything for me or had any respect for me or respect for yourself, you'd move and let me outta here before I start screaming."

Zack moved his hand and opened the door. She looked at his still rock-hard dick, and she left the house with tears streaming down her cheeks.

Ciara banged on the steering wheel. "How could you not know?"

Ciara went straight to her doctor's office. When she arrived at the office, Ciara looked in her rearview mirror.

Her eyes were red from crying. She dug in her purse, got some Visine, and put it in her eyes. Ciara went in and stood anxiously in line and waited to be taken care of.

"I don't see an appointment for you today, Ms. Reynolds," the doctor's receptionist said when it was her turn in line.

"I know. Do you accept walk-ins?"

"Let me see if I can fit you in."

"Thank you," Ciara said, feeling relieved.

"It's going to be a while before the doctor sees you."

"That's all right."

"Can you tell me the nature of today's visit?"

Ciara looked at the reception area and leaned against the counter. "I need to get an AIDS test," Ciara said in a voice barely above a whisper.

"I understand. Please have a seat. I will get you in with his PA. Her name is Hollie Blankenship."

Ciara nodded. "That's fine. I've seen Hollie before."

The receptionist handed her a tablet. "Just a few questions. Just follow the prompts and bring it back to me when you're done."

"Thank you."

Ciara took the tablet and sat down far away from the other patients waiting to see the doctor. That way, she could avoid any conversation about why she was there. Ciara filled out the information on the tablet and reclaimed her seat. She picked up a *Woman's Day* magazine and flipped it open to an article about secrets from star stylists.

Over an hour later, she had read articles on finding joy on the job and a very informative article called "Write This Way" about doing a writing exercise to help delete damaging words and phrases from your inner monologue. The last article Ciara read while she waited to see the PA was titled "Breathe Easy." It recommended some stress-busting ways of breathing to keep you calm even when life gets messy.

"That's me. My life sure has gotten messy today," Ciara said as the doctor's physician's assistant, Hollie Blankenship, came into the reception area.

"Ciara?"

"Yes." Ciara closed the magazine and stood up.

"You can come on back," Hollie said, holding the door open with a welcoming smile.

"Thank you for seeing me," Ciara said and followed Hollie to a patient room.

Once she was in the room, Hollie told her about the procedure for HIV testing.

"I'll draw a blood sample from a vein in your arm, or I'll prick your finger for a small sample. Your choice. I'll collect an oral fluid sample by swabbing your gums to collect the sample of oral fluid."

"I understand." Ciara nodded.

"What happens next is that the sample is sent to a laboratory, and then it's tested for the presence of antibodies or antigens. We do our own rapid testing here on-site, and the results are available within minutes."

"That's what I want."

"Okay. Let's get started. If your test comes back negative, then you do not have HIV. If the test results come back positive, then you do indeed have HIV. If you receive a negative test result, I recommend taking action to prevent HIV."

"Like leaving his gay ass alone."

Hollie smiled. "I think that's a good idea. However, if a rapid test is positive, I'll do a confirmatory blood test to confirm the results. Do you have any questions?"

"No. Let's do it," Ciara said.

Conveniently, she was wearing a sleeveless Victoria Beckham gathered midi dress. Although Ciara didn't mind getting needles since she could remember, she closed her eyes, gritted her teeth, and said, “Ouch,” when Hollie stuck a needle in her right shoulder.

“That’s it.”

Hollie smiled, and she gave her patient a lollipop. *Because who doesn’t love a lollipop?*

“Typically, I’d have your results back within twenty minutes. However, I must tell you that we are a little backed up today, so it might be a little bit longer.”

“I understand,” Ciara said and stood up. “Can I get a grape lollipop, please?”

“Sure thing,” Hollie said. “You can keep the cherry pop, too.”

“Thank you,” Ciara said, and with lollipops in hand, she returned to the waiting room.

Her old seat was taken, so she looked for the person least likely to want to talk, and she sat down next to her.

Ciara chose poorly.

The woman she sat next to talked the entire time she sat there. And her conversation wasn’t about anything remotely interesting, much less important. She complained about everything from the wait to detailing all her issues, and trust, there were a lot of them, and she had plenty of other things to complain about.

Ciara was so glad to see Hollie open the door. “Ciara, you can come on back.”

“Thank you.” Ciara bounced out of her seat and rushed to the patient room behind Hollie.

“I have your results,” Hollie said, looking at the printout in her hand. “You’ll be happy to know that your results came back negative.”

“Overjoyed is more the word I would use.” Ciara bounced up and thought seriously about giving Hollie a hug. She would have if she didn’t think it was inappropriate. “Thank you.”

Ciara left the patient room, and when she passed through the waiting room, she wished her chatty waiting room friend well and headed for home.

On the way, she stopped at her favorite restaurant, Palate Pleasures, and got her favorite comfort food, chicken marsala. Ciara had already decided that she was calling in sick the following day, so when she got her order, she drove to Omelet Oasis and pulled up to the drive-thru. They served breakfast twenty-four hours a day.

"Welcome to Omelet Oasis. What can I get for you today?"

"I'll have a Florentine omelet with spinach and cheese, please."

"Drive forward."

Now that Ciara had her comfort food, she drove home. When she got home, Ciara suddenly felt dirty. Ciara put the Florentine omelet in the refrigerator and the chicken marsala in the microwave and headed for the bathroom, taking her clothes off along the way. She turned on the water, and despite the fact that it was still cold, Ciara got in.

As the water began to get warmer, her tears began to flow again, and she wondered how she didn't know that the man she'd been dating, the man she was engaged to, was gay.

All the signs were there. Ciara simply chose not to see them. Zack got her into watching porno movies while they masturbated. Ciara laughed.

We were both watching the dicks.

Even in that, there were signs. Zack like to watch gangbang or orgy scenes.

More dicks to watch.

Because Zack said that he liked to watch, they would go to underground sex clubs. While they were there, they never had sex with anybody but each other.

As far as you know.

There were a bunch of times that Zack would leave her sitting on a couch masturbating while watching other people having sex. Now, his extended absence brought up questions.

Ain't no telling what or who he was doing.

Then Ciara thought about it.

When Zack did come back, he'd always come back hyped and ready, and since Ciara was hyped and ready from watching, she'd always assumed that he had done the same thing, and they'd have some of their best sex in those clubs.

Now I have to wonder if he brought that dick to me after he fucked some man or some man fucked him.

The biggest clue was Zack's insistence that Ciara allow him to have anal sex with her. She surprised herself that she was into it and now enjoyed anal sex.

"But that is so not the point," she said aloud as her tears continued to flow.

Ciara got out of the shower, dried herself off, put on her comfortable Houston Oilers jersey, and went into the kitchen. She set the microwave to heat up the chicken marsala. She got a glass and looked in the refrigerator for the bottle of wine she cracked open the other day.

"I'm gonna need something a little stronger than that," she said and went to the bar in the living room. "I think Tanqueray will do it."

She had some grapefruit juice in the refrigerator, so Ciara poured herself a drink and sat down to eat her comfort food in her comfort jersey. But it didn't take long before her tears began to flow, and she asked herself the question once again.

"How could you have not known that Zack was gay?"

Chapter Eight

At the end of the day, Savannah said good night to Kiera, and she left the office to meet Thalia at her office to talk about it. That was when they realized that it had been a week since either of them had seen Ciara. She was responding to some texts but had refused any attempt to get together with them for dinner or drinks.

"Something's wrong if Ciara doesn't want to eat or drink," Thalia said.

"I think we should go over there and see what's going on with her," Savannah suggested.

Savannah and Thalia went to Ciara's house. When she opened the door, she was still wearing her Houston Oilers jersey, her hair was matted to her head, and it was obvious from the smell of her that Ciara hadn't bathed. The house was a mess, which was totally out of character for Ciara, who was a bit of a neat freak and kind of anal about it.

"Are you all right?" Thalia asked after they came in and sat down.

Ciara dropped her head. "No. I'm not okay."

"What happened?" Savannah asked.

There was a part of her that didn't want to tell them the truth.

"Zack's been cheating on me."

"Oh, Ciara, I'm sorry," Savannah said.

Thalia looked around the filthy house. "No man is worth this."

"You just don't know, Thalia."

"Yes, she does. You and I both know that Cedric has been cheating on her for years," Savannah said playfully.

Thalia wanted so badly to tell them that she had taken Ciara's "what's good for the goose" suggestion.

Ciara couldn't hold it any longer. "No. Neither of you understand. I went to Zack's house, and I caught him having sex with a man."

"Wait," Savannah said.

"What?" Thalia asked.

"You heard me. Zack is gay."

"Oh, girl, I'm sorry," Savannah said and hugged her, but she was put off because Ciara hadn't bathed.

"That's why he never wanted to set a date for you two to get married. I am so sorry, Ciara."

Savannah stood up. "Come on, stinky."

"What?" Ciara asked.

"When was the last time you bathed?"

"I don't remember, but it's been a couple of days."

"I'll get started cleaning this place up," Thalia said and went into the kitchen to get a garbage bag.

Savannah took Ciara into the bathroom. She turned on the water in the shower. "Come on, strip," Savannah said, holding out her hand as Ciara took off the Oilers jersey. "You know the Oilers haven't played here since 1996, right?"

"What's your point?" Ciara said and stepped into the shower.

"How long have you had this on?"

"Since the day I caught Zack fuckin' another man."

"How long has that been?"

"Since Monday."

"I guess that's why it smells like that," Savannah said, holding the jersey away from herself and putting it in the laundry room. Then Savannah stayed in the bathroom to make sure she washed herself thoroughly.

"You aren't gay, are you, Savannah?"

"No, are you?"

"No, but I was just checking."

While Savannah made sure Ciara bathed, Thalia had straightened up the kitchen and was about to get started cleaning the living room, but she went into the bedroom first.

"My God," she said aloud when she saw that half of the bed had empty or half-full food containers on one side of the bed. She heard the shower running and Savannah and Ciara laughing, and she walked into the bathroom.

"Have you seen this bed?"

"It's a damn shame," Savannah said, shaking her head.

Ciara opened the shower door. "You come home and see Cedric with his dick in another man's ass and see how much you feel like cleaning up." Ciara closed the shower door.

"Apologies," Thalia offered.

"Not saying you aren't right. Just that you need to walk that line before you talk about the repercussions."

"You're right. And once again, I offer my apologies for talking out of school," Thalia said.

"And what are you doing in here?" Ciara asked when she came out of the shower to dry herself.

"She wanted to know if I was gay," Savannah said.

"What did you tell her?"

"I said, 'No, are you?'"

"Get dressed," Thalia said.

"I don't feel like going out," Ciara said as she wrapped a towel around her body and another around her hair because it got wet in the shower.

"We are taking you to the salon to get your hair done. And get a mani-pedi," Thalia said.

"I got a better idea," Savannah said. "I say we go to the spa. We can get a mani-pedi and a massage."

"That does sound good," Ciara said as she went into the bedroom to get changed.

"I thought you had this handled," Savannah said, pointing to the bed.

"We can do that right now while she's getting dressed. Where are your clean sheets, honey?" Thalia asked.

"In the closet in the hall," she called out from her dressing room.

"I got them," Savannah said and went to get the sheets while Thalia stripped the bed.

When Savannah returned with the clean sheets, Ciara was dressed. They made the bed, threw the dirty sheets in the laundry room, and headed for the spa to be pampered.

"Thank you, guys. It is good to have friends like the two of you. Good night," Ciara said when they dropped her off at her house. She went into her house feeling relaxed for the first time in a week. She really needed that, and she was glad that she had friends who cared enough to come see about her and drag her out of the dumps.

But now, she was alone. For the first time in two years, Ciara was alone. She looked at the ring she was still wearing and wondered why. Ciara took off the ring and put it in her jewelry box. What she needed now was to break away from Zack completely.

Ciara went around the house and got everything that belonged to Zack and put it in a trash bag. For a brief moment, she gave some serious thought to getting the ring and throwing it out with the rest of his trash, but Ciara quickly dismissed that idea.

"I need to keep that."

Ciara took the trash bag and put it out on the curb with the rest of the garbage that had been bagged up from around the house. She went back inside and poured herself a glass of Tanqueray and grapefruit juice. Ciara went into the bedroom, turned on her seventy-five-inch television, and went on Pornhub.

What she didn't tell Savannah and Thalia was that she wasn't just lying in bed, ordering takeout for four days. Ciara was lying in bed, ordering takeout, watching porn, and masturbating for four days. It was eat, sleep, masturbate, repeat.

Where Zack preferred the gangbang, orgy, or two guys and one girl, Ciara's preference was two women and one man. Now in light of what was going on in her world, Ciara had to wonder if she was maybe just a little bi-curious.

Ciara took off her clothes, got in bed, and took Ava Vibrator Wand out of the nightstand. Once Pornhub loaded, she typed Ebony Lesbian. The clip Ciara found was Coworkers August Skye and Ana Foxxx Have Finger Butt Massage from Masseuse Destiny Mira.

"That sounds hot."

And it was.

Ciara watched, squeezed her breasts and her nipples, and Ava Vibrator Wand did the rest. She came and came hard. It was so hard that it made her head spin.

"That was powerful."

But Ciara still liked watching dicks, so she decided to close out the evening's session with one of her favorites. When Zack wasn't able to make her cum and then pass out, Ciara would break out Ava Vibrator, turn on Pornhub, and watch two women having sex with one man.

However, her favorite was with Jada Fire, Jasmine Cashmere, and some guy whose name she never knew. Now, in light of everything going on in her world, Ciara wondered what that said about her.

Because you sure do like watching Jada Fire. But so did Zack. He was the one who turned me on to Jada Fire.

Then she thought about it. *Jada Fire will be with two, sometimes three men at a time. More dicks for him to watch. And it would have seemed suspicious if he knew the names of the male porn stars the way he knew the women.*

Ciara shook her head and started the clip.

Without Zack's fragile ego lying next to her, she masturbated, and she screamed like a banshee.

Ciara had just put Ava back in the nightstand and turned off the television when she got a text from Rahim. Ciara hadn't heard from him since the night they went out to dinner.

The text was simple.

Hi.

Hi, yourself. It's been a while. How have you been?

I've been great. Wanted to know if you were free for dinner tomorrow.

I'm free right now if you want to get together.

I would love to get together.

I'm texting you my address.

Ciara sent Rahim her address.

Got it! I'll see you in about an hour.

Looking forward to seeing you.

Ciara got out of bed and opened her sexy lingerie drawer and selected a Kiki de Montparnasse sheer lace midi dress. Just in case the invitation to come over to her house at ten o'clock wasn't enough, the sight of her in sheer lace with nothing on under it should let him know that she meant business.

Since she had just spent the last hour masturbating, Ciara got in the shower, moisturized her body with coco butter, and sprayed on some Jimmy Choo perfume.

When Ciara opened the door to let Rahim into the house, and he saw what she was wearing, he took a deep breath.

"You are so beautiful, Ciara," he said, taking her into his arms and kissing her.

Ciara felt the passion in his kiss. It felt like Rahim had real affection and desire for her. She felt herself getting wetter from his kiss as his hands began to slowly roam over her body. He pulled the thin straps of the sheer lace gown and cupped her breasts in his big palms before leaning forward to suck on each nipple.

Ciara let the gown fall to the floor. Rahim started to undress in front of her. She sat down on the couch and watched in anxious anticipation as he took his time getting naked. And then the moment of truth arrived, and he took his dick out.

"You're so big," Ciara said as Rahim stood in front of her. "So fucking big. And I love a big dick." Ciara took his dick in her hand and stroked it before taking it to the back of her throat.

"I gotta say, I wasn't expecting this when I sent you that text."

"Sometimes things work out better than we expect," Ciara stopped sucking long enough to say.

"True."

Rahim reached out, grabbed her head, and ran his fingers through her hair. Then he began gently massaging Ciara's swollen bud.

"That feels so good," she cried out as Rahim knelt between her legs.

He pulled her closer so he was in a perfect position to ease his tongue inside of Ciara. Rahim held her thighs apart, nibbling, suckling, and flicking against her bud.

"Right there. Don't you dare stop!" Ciara screamed. "You're gonna make me cum!"

After she came hard, Ciara pushed his head away and stood up.

"Come on," she said, grabbing him by the hand and leading him into the bedroom.

He lay on the bed and tried to pull Ciara down on top of him. She straddled his lap, grabbed his dick, and slowly lowered herself onto him, enjoying being in control. When she and Zack had sex, it had to be all his way.

Ciara moved her body up and down on him, grinding her hips into him with each stroke. Rahim was slamming his dick in her hard and fast, so Ciara stepped up her pace a couple notches. She rolled off of him and got on her knees.

Rahim quickly fell in behind her and pounded away from behind. He was hitting it so hard that it came out. Ciara grabbed it, spun around quickly, sucked it, and just as quickly got back on her knees and carefully guided his dick into her ass.

"Oh, shit."

Rahim's dick was bigger and thicker than Zack's, so it took her a minute to adjust to his size, but soon Ciara increased her pace and began slamming her body into him with everything she had.

He reached for her shoulders and pounded Ciara. In response, she began winding her hips until he let go of her shoulders. Trying to maintain his control, he quickly grabbed her hips.

Ciara was bucking her ass into him so hard that he had let go. Ciara began to buck harder and harder until Ciara felt her entire body start to tremble.

Ciara screamed, "Fuck me!" at the top of her lungs.

Chapter Nine

After thinking about it for a week and starting and stopping three times, Thalia created an account on Black People Come Together. Now that she created the account, she had to select an image. Thalia looked through the pictures that she had and looked for one that didn't make her look like a thirty-something mother of three. She ran across an image of her, Savannah, and Ciara that was taken at a gala event that Zack had tickets to. That night, Thalia was wearing a red Et Ochs Victoria ruched jersey halter A-line gown.

The gown was sleeveless and backless, so that night she wasn't wearing a bra, and since Thalia was heavy chested, she didn't think the dress would support her. However, Thalia looked amazing. Her hair and makeup were professionally done. The only problem was that Savannah and Ciara were in the picture. However, there was enough space between her and Ciara that she could crop them out. Once that was done, Thalia shut down her computer and went to cook dinner for the children.

Once she cleaned up the kitchen and saw that the children were doing what they were supposed to be doing, she got back to her new online dating account. Thalia was pleasantly surprised to find that her inbox was filled with messages from men. She excitedly read them all. Without exception, all of them said how fine and sexy she looked in that red dress. The good ones, the ones that had potential, she read twice.

Thalia picked the one who seemed to match her interests. He wasn't a bad-looking man, and she began a dialogue with Griffin Vaughan. According to his dating profile, he was a medical assistant at a local hospital.

They exchanged messages for two weeks, and that was when the messages turned into sex messages. Each one described in graphic detail what they would do and wanted to be done when they got together.

When I see you, I'm going to take my time and undress you slowly. Once you were naked, I would take the opportunity to sit and admire how fine you look. Then I would back you up to the nearest wall, and I'd start at your feet and kiss my way up. Your sexy calves, your thighs, until I reach the wetness between those thighs. I would massage your clit with my finger before I licked and sucked it until I brought you to an earth-shattering, screaming orgasm.

After that earth-shattering, screaming orgasm, I would need to sit down to catch myself. I would sit on the edge of the bed, and I'd call you over. Once you were standing in front of me, I would stand up just long enough to unbutton your shirt and ease it off those broad shoulders. Then I would sit down, unbuckle your belt, pull down your zipper so you can come out of those pants. And once you were standing before me naked, I would take that big dick you say you have and run my tongue up and down your shaft until it starts to throb before I put it in my mouth.

After a week of sex messaging on Black People Come Together, arrangements were made for them to get together.

"Why don't you meet me at Hampton Inn on JFK Boulevard?" Thalia suggested.

She didn't have time to be wined and dined. She wanted to have sex, pick up the children from her neighbor, go home, and cook dinner.

“That will be okay,” Griffin said.

“Call me when you get there, and I’ll tell you what room I’m in.”

“Sounds good. I’ll see you tonight, Thalia. I’m looking forward to it.”

“So am I.”

When Thalia ended the call, she thought she heard the relieved sound in his voice. It was as if he was going to suggest it and she saved him the trouble. That was the first time that she thought that Griffin might be married too. And if that were the case, it was even better. If they were both married, they would both be into the hit-and-run, “have some fun” mentality.

“If it’s good, of course.”

When Thalia checked into the room, she took a shower and put on a red Eberjey satin and lace cut-out back chemise before she called Griffin to tell him what room she was in. He was parked in the lot, waiting for her call.

“I’ll be right up.”

When he knocked on the door, Thalia stood up, and she went to open it.

“Hello,” Griffin said.

“Hello, yourself. You want to come in?”

He looked at Thalia in that chemise. “Very much.”

When she stepped aside and let him in, Thalia closed the door behind him. All the things that each one wrote about how they intended to take their time undressing the other slowly, there would be none of that. The second the door was closed, they were in each other’s arms, kissing and trying frantically to come out of those clothes. Once they were naked, they kissed their way to the bed. Thalia pushed Griffin on the bed.

“I want to feel you inside me.”

Thalia crawled up on the bed and ran her hands over his chest. Griffin watched as her tongue moved softly across his chest. The sensation of her tongue flicking his nipple made his entire body quiver. She looked into his eyes and lost herself in the passion that burned so intensely in them. She ran her finger along her lips and licked it before gliding that moistened finger down her cleavage, and then she moistened her finger again and used it to rub her stiffened nipples while staring directly into his eyes.

"You're driving me insane," Griffin said.

Thalia massaged her nipple with one hand—and then, very slowly, she began to finger her clit with the other.

"Damn."

Griffin squeezed her breasts together and relished them with his tongue. She ran her hands all over his body, and then she knelt on the bed. Her head felt as if it were spinning as she sucked his dick. It was as if it were all happening in slow motion.

Thalia looked at his erection, which was standing as straight as the Washington Monument.

"Damn, you got a big dick," she whispered. "And I love a big dick."

Thalia clasped her fingers together and placed them around his throbbing dick. Slowly but ever so firmly, she moved her hands up and down. She began to fondle his balls with one hand and stroked him with the other.

Thalia licked her lips as she felt his dick swelling in her hand. His balls were getting fat, too, so she squeezed them lightly, let go of his dick, and lowered her head to his throbbing dick. Griffin propped a pillow behind his head and watched Thalia as her tongue slid up and down his dick. With her thumb and forefinger, she squeezed the bottom of his shaft, causing his head to swell. Thalia ran circles around his head with her tongue. Griffin tried to reach for her, but she wouldn't stop what she was doing.

She ran her tongue over her lips and gently kissed his head, then slid her moistened lips down on him. Up and down, deeper and deeper, slowly, until she had taken almost all of him in her mouth. Thalia could tell by the look on his face that Griffin was in ecstasy.

His body became tense and rigid, and Thalia felt him begin to expand inside her mouth as she licked and sucked him. She could tell he was getting ready to come, so she stopped, squeezed his dick in her hand, and felt it twitching.

"I'm not ready for you to come yet," Thalia said, lying next to him, spreading her legs. "Come here."

Thalia straddled Griffin. She wiggled her hips and moved her body slowly, making love like they were made for one another.

Thalia tried to roll off Griffin, but he would have none of that. It felt so good, sliding in and out of her, that he didn't ever want her to stop. She was moving her body from side to side, rubbing her nipples across his chest. Thalia could tell that Griffin was in ecstasy. He grabbed her ass, and she started to move her hips faster.

She felt his dick expand and pushed it into her harder. Her body began to shake. She moved her body up and down, grinding her hips into him with each stroke. As Thalia drenched Griffin with her juices, she leaned forward and kissed him excitedly while she continued to ride him harder. Griffin sucked her nipple harder, and her mouth opened wide.

"I'm cumming!" she yelled, and her head drifted back.

She rolled off Griffin and got up on her knees. He stood up, stroked his erection, got behind her, grabbed her hips, and entered her. She was so wet, and he was so hard that Griffin began to pump it in her as hard as he could.

"Give it to me harder. I wanna feel all of you in me."

Griffin reached for her shoulders, pounding his dick into her, and he felt her cum again. The feeling of her wall spasming around his dick felt amazing, and he came with force, hollering, “Yes!”

“That shit was intense,” he said.

“It was great,” Thalia breathed out.

And thc second it was over, Griffin jumped up and headed for the shower.

“Save some hot water,” Thalia said and glanced at the clock next to the bed.

She had an hour before she had to pick up the children. Thalia relaxed and basked in the afterglow of amazing sex. Once Griffin got out of the shower and got dressed, she got out of bed and walked him to the door. Thalia took a shower, got dressed, and went to pick up her children, and they went home. She cooked dinner, and they were eating when Cedric came home.

Chapter Ten

With everyone having such busy schedules, it had been almost a month since all three friends had gotten together. And since that wouldn't do, they met at a lounge called Sizzle Fusion.

"How have you been, Savannah?" Ciara asked.

"I've been okay. I'm adjusting to being alone for the first time in my life. I went from my parents' house, went to college, got pregnant, and got married. I've never been alone before, and it takes getting used to."

"You're making me feel like a bad friend," Thalia said.

"Yeah, me too," Ciara concurred.

"Why? You two have been great through all of this. We've hung out. This might be the first time in a while for the three of us. But when it's over, I still have to go home to the big, empty house. No husband, no kids, just me." Savannah smiled. "But I'm adjusting."

"Now that we're both single women, we need to get out more," Ciara said. "I'll be your wing woman."

"I hear you. And we really should do that. But my divorce date is coming up in two weeks. And I've got too much going on at the office to give up that kind of energy."

"Just an idea. You're a young, beautiful woman, Savannah. You need to get back out there," Ciara encouraged.

"I know. And you're right."

"I have something to tell y'all," Thalia said. "I set up an account on the dating app Black People Come Together."

"Good for you," Ciara said. "Have you met anybody interesting?"

"I've been messaging with a couple of guys." Thalia paused. "But I've met one of them."

"Ooh, girl, details," Savannah said, thinking that maybe she should set up an account on one of those sites. Perhaps she could find one that catered to single Black female executives.

"His name is Griffin Vaughan."

"Well, let's see him," Ciara said, and Thalia logged into Black People Come Together and saw that she had a message from Griffin. She went to his profile.

"That's him," Thalia said and showed her girls his picture.

"He's a good-looking man," Ciara said.

"When you said you met him," Savannah began, "did you meet him, meet him?"

"Yes, Savannah. I met him, met him." She leaned forward. "And I fucked him, fucked him," Thalia said, and there were high-fives all around. "What's good for the goose is now great for the gander."

Thalia checked the message she got from Griffin. It said that he was free for a few hours and wanted to know if she could slip away. "In fact, this is him now, wanting to get together."

"You should go," Savannah encouraged.

"Yes, Thalia, you should go. One of us needs to be getting some," Ciara said.

"We're your alibi if you need one."

"Y'all sure?"

"Yes," Savannah said, and Ciara nodded. "Go!" they both said.

When Thalia was gone, Ciara got a call from Zack. They hadn't seen or spoken to each other since she caught him with another man. Since then, he had been calling and texting Ciara, insisting that he could explain.

"We just need to talk. Please call me. I'm just so lost without you, Ciara." And he would always end by saying, "I love you."

How could you not know Zack was gay? And what does that say about you as a woman? Ciara asked herself over and over again.

"Savannah?"

Savannah turned to see who spoke to her with a voice so deep that she felt it at her core. "Milo? Milo Henderson," Savannah said, and then she smiled.

Milo Henderson went to college with Savannah. She got up and hugged him. It felt good to be in a man's arms again. Since Greyson walked out of her life and their marriage, she hadn't been seeing anybody. Her reasoning was that she had too much going on at Intuitive Energy and she didn't have the time or the energy to cultivate and maintain a relationship.

The truth was much simpler than that.

She was in love with Greyson. After all those years, Savannah still loved the man she married. She had no idea, because he never expressed it, that he felt emasculated by her success.

"How have you been, Savannah?"

"I've been great. What about you?"

"I'm good. Doing really well for myself."

"Milo, this is my friend Ciara. Milo and I went to Texas Southern together."

"It's nice to meet you, Milo," Ciara said, and she leaned closer to Savannah. "He is fine," she whispered. "You need to fuck him before he leaves H-Town." Ciara got up and went to the bar. "Excuse me."

"I didn't mean to run your friend off."

"She'll be back."

"What about you?" Milo asked. "What have you been up to since college?"

"I'm the president of Intuitive Energy."

"Wow. You've been doing very well. But I always knew you would be successful at whatever you did."

"What about you? What have you been doing since our college days?"

"I'm a major account executive with Quanti 6."

"Quanti 6." Savannah nodded. "I've heard of them."

"Naturally, I've heard of Intuitive Energy. It was one of the hundred best companies to work for in America."

"Was."

He leaned close to her. "Do I hear a note of discontent in your voice?"

"You do. But that's my issue."

"I understand." Milo nodded.

"So, major account executive with Quanti 6. Is that what brings you to Houston?"

"Yes. I'm here meeting my client for dinner tonight. I'll be here a couple of days, and then I'm going back to New York after that."

"New York. That's where you're from, right?"

"You remembered."

"I remember a lot about you from those days."

"You do?" Milo asked. But instead of asking Savannah what she remembered about him, Milo asked the question he had wanted to ask since the second he saw her. "Where's Greyson tonight?"

Savannah's entire facial expression changed from a beautiful smile to a frown. "I don't know where Greyson is. Greyson and I are getting divorced."

Milo smiled because that was exactly what he wanted to hear.

"But you should reach out to him. I can give you his number so you guys can catch up."

"No, Savannah, I don't think so. I'm catching up with the person I want to catch up with."

"Okay. I thought you and Greyson were cool."

Milo laughed. "Whatever gave you that idea?"

"I don't know. I just thought you guys were cool."

"I guess we were cool. But . . ."

"But what?"

"I have a confession to make."

"What's that?"

Milo leaned forward and looked into Savannah's eyes. "I had a huge crush on you since I first saw you on the first day of freshman orientation. I was going to step to you, but Greyson was faster."

Savannah smiled.

"What are you smiling about?" Milo needed to know.

"Because I have a confession to make."

"What's that?"

"I was looking at you the same way at freshman orientation. But like you said, Greyson was faster."

"Wow." Milo sat back and let his brain wrap around that for a second or two. "So, I spent the next four years watching you from a distance. Watching you be happy with Greyson. Even though I was desperately in love with you. All I wanted was for you to be happy."

"I thought I was happy. But I was wrong."

Savannah dropped her head in sadness. Then her smile returned, and she looked up at Milo. "What about you? You ever get married?"

"Do you remember Kimberley Swanson?"

"You and she got together our senior year. You married her?"

"And she divorced me three years ago."

"I'm sorry."

"I'm not."

"Then I'm not either." Savannah laughed. "Any kids?"

"Two. A boy and a girl."

"You got any pictures?"

"Of course I do," Milo said, reaching into his pocket for his phone. "What about you?" he asked, and Savannah dug in her purse and got her phone.

After the two compared pictures of their children, Milo asked the question that he wanted to ask since Savannah said that she was getting divorced. "Are you doing anything tomorrow evening?"

"No, I have no plans for tomorrow."

"I would love it if you'd join me for dinner."

"It would be my pleasure."

"There's a pan-Latin steak house, Toro Toro, in the hotel where I'm staying." It was then that Milo's client arrived. "There's my guy. Tell Ciara it was nice meeting her." Milo took Savannah's hand in his. "I will see you tomorrow."

"I'm looking forward to it."

Ciara saw Milo go off with his client, and she returned to the table with Savannah. "Oh, no, you didn't let Mr. Sexy leave without you getting some," Ciara said when she sat down.

"We're having dinner at his hotel tomorrow night. So, yes, I plan to fuck him before he leaves H-Town."

"Good for you."

"What about you? You getting any?" Savannah asked and hoped that she didn't say that she was back with Zack.

"You remember me telling you about a guy I'd been exchanging text messages with? His name is Rahim Dalton."

"Vaguely."

"We got together. Nothing serious. I just needed to release the pressure."

"Believe me, I understand," Savannah said, and her plan was to seek a release from all the pent-up pressures she was carrying around daily.

The following evening, Savannah went to the Four Seasons Hotel to meet Milo for dinner at Toro Toro. Over Peruvian grilled chicken and zarandeado red snapper, they talked about life as Black executives, their children, and the highlights and lowlights of their failed marriages.

Then Savannah asked the question that she wanted to ask since the words came flying out of his mouth. “So you were desperately in love with me?”

“Yes.” Milo chuckled. “I remember times when we were at the same place at the same time. I would just sit and watch you sometimes.”

“Now, you see, after all these years, I wasn’t crazy.” Savannah smiled brightly. “I would feel you looking at me, but when I’d look at you—”

“I’d be looking somewhere else.”

“Yes.”

“You had a tell.”

“What was my tell?” She giggled like a schoolgirl. “I’m dying to hear this.”

“You would always hesitate before you looked,” Milo said and demonstrated the move for her.

Savannah leaned forward. “Did you ever notice that when I did look, I didn’t look away when I saw you weren’t looking at me?”

“I thought you were just trying to catch me when I got back to looking at you.”

“I had two children while I was at Texas Southern.”

“And you had that beautiful pregnant woman glow.” Milo sat back and picked up his drink. “What do you think, you’re going to talk me out of it now?” He leaned forward. “I fell in love with you the first time I saw you at freshmen orientation.” He laughed. “And to know that all I had to be was faster because you were digging me too. It’s making me think that I am not going to let this just be a chance meeting.”

"What are you prepared to do to make that happen?" Savannah asked and hoped whatever he had in mind included him making love to her.

It had been ages since she'd had sex with anyone other than herself since Greyson walked out and ended their twenty-year marriage. The excuse she used was that she was too busy dealing with her new position. Savannah looked across the table at Milo. He was still just as fine as he was when they were in college.

"I hope I'm not being too forward." Milo paused, and then he chuckled. "Yes, I am being forward. I'm staying here at the hotel."

"You did mention that."

"Will you join me for a drink in my room? Please say yes."

"Yes."

Milo looked around the restaurant and raised his hand. "Check, please."

Soon, Savannah joined Milo in the premier executive suite, but they never did get around to having that drink. It didn't take long before they were both naked, and Milo was sliding his hands across her chest, admiring the softness of her skin, before taking one of Savannah's nipples into his mouth.

Savannah leaned back against the headboard, held Milo's head in place with one hand, and squeezed her breast with the other. Savannah took his face into her hands and kissed him gently. Their kiss was long and tender, and his tongue felt like it was overpowering hers, bending her to his will. Savannah gladly submitted.

Milo looked at Savannah. To him, she was still the most beautiful woman he had ever seen. He had loved her for so long, and to finally have her in his arms was nothing short of mind-blowing.

Milo crawled between Savannah's legs and very deliberately spread her lips with his thumb and forefinger while making small circles around her clit with the tip of his finger. Milo rubbed her swollen clit. Savannah was drenched from all that he was making her feel. There were no words that could describe the sensation that she felt when Milo sucked her moist lips gently and slid his tongue inside of her.

Savannah felt her body quiver as Milo licked her clit with the tip of his tongue, weaving magic that she felt at her core. Her head drifted back as the circles he made built the tension inside before making her explode. Savannah's thighs pressed together as her body convulsed uncontrollably.

Milo lay there next to Savannah. She began gliding her hand up and down his erection. Savannah got up on the bed and eased herself down on it. She moaned her pleasure while continuing to slide up and down on his shaft. The feeling got her so caught up that Savannah slammed her body against his in anxious anticipation of each stroke.

Determined to bring them both to climax together, Savannah rode him harder, working her hips and inner muscles until he couldn't hold back any longer. When he began to swell and explode inside of her, Savannah collapsed on his chest while she continued working her hips and inner muscles.

Chapter Eleven

Savannah was in her office when Kiera informed her that Fatima Camacho from the legal department was here to see her.

"Did she say what it was in reference to?" Savannah asked as she looked out her window. It really had become the best thing about working there. When she looked out that window, Savannah felt peaceful, and for a short time, her life was just a little less chaotic.

"No. Do you want me to ask?"

"No. Send her in." Savannah spun around in her chair as Fatima Camacho walked into her office.

"Good afternoon, Savannah. I'm Fatima Camacho," she said with her hand out. Savannah stood up and shook hands. "I'm from the legal department."

"Please, have a seat. And tell me what I can do for you."

"I know you're wondering what somebody from the legal department wants with you."

"You're right. I was wondering that very thing."

"I can imagine. But this visit is informational only."

"Information is good."

"I came to inform you that a former Intuitive Energy executive, Kiran Caldwell, is going to be sentenced today. She was charged with criminal insider trading."

"What did she do?"

"Caldwell sold fifty thousand shares of Intuitive Energy stock when the stock price dipped from its high of ninety dollars per share to seventy-five per share a week before the fifty-million-dollar loss was reported."

"That was three years ago."

"It won't affect you in any way. At most you'll be asked to comment on it by reporters."

"And do I have a response, or is my response 'no comment'?"

"I will provide your assistant with the prepared statement. It basically says that it occurred before your tenure at Intuitive Energy. Other than that, you have no comment."

"I can do that."

All this went on three years before Savannah came to Intuitive Energy as its president. When the loss was reported, as he did many times before, Brodrick Fowler issued a statement in which investors were advised to hold steady or continue buying Intuitive Energy stock because the stock price would rebound shortly.

However, Savannah had noted some of the same things that Brodrick was doing to steady investors when the stock price dipped. Therefore, when asked to comment on the sentencing, Savannah gave the prepared response.

"That occurred before my tenure as president at Intuitive Energy. Other than that, I have no comment."

And when reporters asked about the falling stock price, her response was, once again, the company line. As company president, Savannah repeated the company line, as did the members of the board and other senior executives at Intuitive Energy.

"Investors should continue to buy stock or hold steady if they already owned Intuitive Energy because the stock price will rebound."

It was the official Intuitive Energy position.

Where it was Fowler three years ago, now it was Savannah who was called upon to grant a selected reporter an interview about the strength of projected third-quarter earnings. In addition, she was urged to issue a statement, and she held a press conference repeating the company line. She could always hear Fowler's voice in the back of her mind.

"In order for this to work, you and I have to be in perfect tune. Walking the same walk, talking the same talk."

"You're friends with Ciara Reynolds?" Fatima asked to bring Savannah out of her thoughts.

"Ciara Reynolds. Yes, I've known her for years."

"She's a good attorney. If you're as smart as I think you are, and I think you are, you've already spoken with her about some of the things you've learned in the last seven months."

"I have."

Fatima nodded, and then she gathered her papers. "Don't put her on retainer." She stood up. "There are certain people who get nervous when people seek outside counsel."

"I understand."

Fatima stopped at the door. "Find ways to protect yourself, Savannah."

Fatima's visit made Savannah wonder about Kiran Caldwell, what she was charged with, and about the reported loss. She remembered that in her research about the $50 million loss, she had found an old article by Salma Ho noting that no one understood how the company made money and questioned whether Intuitive Energy stock was overvalued. Just as some analysts were doing now.

As it got closer to five in the afternoon, Kiera said good night and left for the day. That left Savannah alone with the voice of Fatima Camacho from the legal department replacing that of Brodrick Fowler.

"Find ways to protect yourself, Savannah."

She got her purse from the desk drawer and headed for the private elevator she shared with Brodrick. Once Savannah was out of the building, she took out her cell phone and called Ciara to see if she had time to meet her. Ciara said that she was at her house and Savannah was welcome to come by.

"As long as you bring dinner."

"What do you want to eat?"

"I was thinking Mexican."

"Any place in particular?"

"You remember that place Thalia took us to? What was the name of it?"

"I remember that the food was good, but I don't remember the name or where to find it."

"You on your way here?"

"Yes."

"I'll call Thalia, find out where this place is, and I'll know by the time you get here."

"You want me to pick you up, I take it?"

"You take it correctly. I wanna ride in the limo," Ciara said as the limousine driver opened the door and Savannah got in.

Once she picked up Ciara, who immediately poured herself a glass of champagne, the driver took them to La Cocina Fiesta.

"Thalia is going to meet us there," Ciara informed.

"I was hoping she would."

When they all arrived at La Cocina Fiesta, they talked about what was going on at Intuitive Energy and Fatima Camacho's warning for Savannah to protect herself.

"I know a guy who works white collar crimes at the FBI. I talked to him when I first mentioned it to you, and he said to reach out when you're ready. I think now would be a good time for you to reach out."

"Can you do that for me?"

"No problem. In fact, it'll be better coming from me. I can be there with you when you meet him if you like."

"Would you?"

"Of course."

"If I had a reason to be there, I would be there with you too," Thalia said as their server brought a platter with chilaquiles, tacos, burritos, tamales, quesadillas, enchiladas, and nogada peppers because Ciara liked it spicy.

"Of course you have a reason to be there. Not only are you one of my two best friends, but you are my financial advisor. A lot of what's going on over there has to do with their accounting practices. So, yes, Thalia, you need to be present and accounted for at this meeting."

"I'll arrange it," Ciara said and began filling her plate. The first thing she grabbed was a nogada pepper.

"Talk about something," Savannah requested as she put a quesadilla and a burrito on her plate. "What's going on in your world, Ciara?"

"I've got a trial to prepare for later this month." She took a bite of her tamale. "And I'm taking over an account from another attorney at the firm, so I'm flying to Saint Barts to review the client's reports."

"Saint Barts," Thalia said. "I'm jealous. All I got coming up is a company that hired us to audit his company as a result of a Medicare inquiry."

"That does not sound nearly as exciting as flying to Saint Barts, Thalia. I understand why you're jealous. I know I am."

"Sorry, ladies, I wish I could bring you along, but . . ." She paused. "You should get a room at a resort."

"I pass," Savannah said. "Not that I wouldn't want to, but I really do have a lot going on right now."

“Same here. I got this audit coming up. It may not be as exciting as flying off to Saint Barts, but it pays excellent money.”

“And it is all about the money,” Ciara said.

“Tell me about it,” Savannah said. All her issues were about the money.

Chapter Twelve

Thalia was at the Hampton Inn on JFK Boulevard for another meetup with Griffin. When he arrived, Griffin apologized for being a little late getting there. Thalia was about to accept his apology and talk about how bad traffic was in some places before his mouth covered hers, and their tongues intertwined. Griffin lifted her Erdem gathered floral midi skirt and maneuvered his hand between her thighs.

Thalia's legs spread, and she kissed him passionately and began to stroke his erection. She unbuttoned her blouse and unhooked her bra. Griffin squeezed her breasts and relished them with his tongue. Thalia started making circles around his nipples, and his body shook. She moved closer to Griffin and pressed her body against his. She took off his pants and got on top of him, but Griffin flipped her over gently.

Griffin reached between her legs and fingered her clit with one hand and squeezed her breast with the other.

"Take me, Griffin," she whispered in his ear and spread her legs.

Griffin knelt on the bed. He began to massage her thighs, allowing his hands to flow freely all over Thalia's body.

"You are so beautiful."

Griffin trapped her swollen clit in the gap between his teeth. The louder Thalia moaned, the harder Griffin sucked. She rocked her hips, and Griffin slowly inserted two of his fingers inside of her. In and out—slowly and deliberately, he probed in search of her G-spot.

Once he found it, Thalia felt like her eyeballs were about to explode.

"Ooooh, Griffin, I like it like that."

Griffin eased himself inside Thalia. She moaned and squirmed as she took in every inch of him. Then she began working her hips and inner muscles while licking his nipples. Thalia's plump ass was jiggling back at him. Thalia spread her legs, and he entered her with force.

"You are so hard for me!" Thalia shouted.

Her words made Griffin slam his body into Thalia with everything he had.

"Fuck me harder!" she screamed, and her muscles tightened around him. "Oh, shit! I'm about to . . . I'm about to . . . Oh, shit!"

And when it was over, as he did the last time they got together, as soon as it was over, Griffin got out of bed quickly, kissed Thalia on her cheek, and headed for the bathroom to shower. Thalia hadn't noticed it when he came into the room, but Griffin had a small bag, which he grabbed on the way to the shower.

When he came out of the bathroom, Griffin grabbed the clothes from the floor that he took off during a frantic and frenzied rush to be inside her. As he got dressed, Thalia glanced at the clock next to the bed. She told her neighbor, Mrs. Johnson, that she would pick up her kids at six, so she wasn't in a rush to run to the shower.

"Mind if I ask you a question?" Thalia asked Griffin as he hurried to get dressed.

"You can ask me anything. What's up?"

"Are you married?"

Griffin stopped getting dressed and sat at the far edge of the bed just in case Thalia was mad enough about him being married to take a swing at him. It'd happened before.

"Yes, Thalia, I'm married. Does that bother you?"

"Not at all. I'm married as well. Go ahead and get dressed and get out of here, and I'll see you next time you're available."

He hopped up from the bed and kissed Thalia, finished getting dressed, kissed her again, and got out of there because he had gone way over the time he said he'd be home.

When she got home, Thalia went next door to pick up her children from her neighbor's house. However, Mrs. Johnson once again told her that they weren't there.

"Your husband came and picked them up about an hour ago. He said something about going to Arby's because 'they have the meats.'"

"Okay," she laughed and went home.

Who knew all I had to do was cheat on him to get him to spend more time with his children?

Consequently, Thalia went home and took advantage of the quiet house to take a long, hot bath. As she soaked, she sipped a glass of Tiberio Pecorino wine and replayed the finer moments of her evening with Griffin.

She closed her eyes and could see and actually feel Griffin pulling her hips up and slamming himself as hard as he could into Thalia. She grabbed the sheets. Her face was pressed into the bed. Thalia could feel her nipples stiffen as they were smashed into the mattress. Just the thought of it made her entire body tremble.

When Cedric got home from Arby's with their children, he found his wife in their bedroom getting dressed after coming out of the bathtub.

"Where you been?"

"I had a meeting with a client for cocktails and a conversation about his account," Thalia said and proceeded to tell Cedric an entirely fictional story about how the meeting went, just as he did to her many times when he'd come home after sleeping with another woman.

"Oh, okay," Cedric said.

"Thanks for picking up the children."

"No problem. And, just so you know, Aliza doesn't like Mrs. Johnson."

"She doesn't?"

"Nope. She calls me every time you drop them off over there." Cedric glanced at his watch. "I need to change this suit."

"Why? Where are you going?"

"I gotta meet Trystan Gillespie."

"Who is he?"

"A new client I'm trying to land," he said, and while he got dressed, Cedric told Thalia an entirely fictional story about what the potential client's business was and how they did business.

"Okay," Thalia said and stood up.

Once Cedric was dressed, she walked him to the door and gave him a kiss.

"I'll see you when you get back." Thalia pressed her body against him. "I'll have it wet and ready for you to get back to."

Cedric kissed Thalia. "You know I like that fat, juicy pussy wet."

"I know you do. That's why I do it. Go on and get outta here."

"I won't be gone long," Cedric lied.

He was going to spend some time with Lula Mendoza. She was a young, hot Mexican woman who liked to ride as if she were a wild cowgirl in heat, and she could go all night.

After the children went to sleep, Thalia went online and saw that she had a message from Aston Hoover. He came right out and told Thalia that he was married.

"Is that gonna be a problem for us?"

"No, because I'm married too."

Since she was already involved with Griffin and he was married, one more married man didn't make much of a difference to her. They had exchanged messages for about a month now.

That night, as they had been, Thalia and Aston were sending a series of sexually charged, graphic sexual messages. The messages were so hot that they had Thalia on edge.

We need to get together right now and explore this passion.

You know I can't do that. I have my children. And I am not the kind of woman to leave her kids home alone to get some dick.

I know. I've known a few of them who do it all the time.

I bet you have.

I know it's late, and you can't leave because you got your kids.

True.

How about I come over there and make circles around that fat, throbbing clit you say you got in the car? Then, you can go back inside, curl into the fetal position, and go to sleep.

The idea of it excited her. Thalia had never done anything close to that. Prior to becoming a woman who cheated on her husband with married men, she was quite conservative, careful, and methodical, as her training and experience in accounting had shaped what she did and how she thought and saw things. This involved risk. *Suppose I get caught.* And it was that risk that made it exciting.

Come on.

Thalia gave him her address and shut down her laptop. She took a minute to think about what would happen if she were in the driveway screaming when Cedric decided to come home from having sex with whoever the lucky woman was that night.

I'll deal with that when it happens.

Right then, she took a shower to be fresh and ready for Aston to make her cum. When he arrived, Thalia came outside. They introduced themselves since this was the first time they'd met in person. Then Aston opened the back door of his car, and Thalia got in.

Soon Aston's lips and tongue were engaged with her lips and clit, slowly tonguing her lips and sucking lightly on her clit. Thalia spread her legs a little wider and held his head in place. Her head drifted back, and she felt her body begin to quiver.

"Oh, yes! Oh, my God, yes!" she screamed.

When it was over, Thalia said good night to Aston with a promise to get together soon. She had just closed the door when Cedric's car pulled into their driveway. Thalia rushed into the bathroom and did a quick wash, jumped in bed, and played asleep as Cedric came into the room and into the bathroom and did a quick wash before he got in bed with Thalia.

"You asleep?"

"Not anymore."

They talked for a while about the client meeting, and then they had the most amazing sex she'd ever had. While Cedric was deep inside, making her walls clench and release around him, she was thinking about the sex she'd had with Griffin earlier that evening and with Aston just minutes before her husband came home. She'd never had sex with three men on the same day. In fact, the only man Thalia had sex with since the day they met and she fell in love was Cedric.

Chapter Thirteen

Savannah felt as if she'd been blindsided when she read an article written by an energy market expert. The article was: INTUITIVE ENERGY IS ALL DRESSED UP AND NOWHERE TO GO BUT DOWN.

The article encouraged investors to sell Intuitive Energy stock, although the article only changed the recommendation on the stock from "buy" to "neutral."

She was informed that later that day, Brodrick Fowler was going to have a press conference, and he wanted her to be there. She was to stand there behind him while he reassured investors that the stock would rebound.

By that time, Intuitive Energy's stock price had decreased from its high of $90 a share to $74 a share. However, investors still trusted Brodrick Fowler and believed him when he said that Intuitive Energy would once again rule the market.

"Technical Support, this is Dylan speaking. How can I help you?"

"Good afternoon, Dylan, it's Savannah. Can you come to my office when you have a minute? I need you to do something for me, please."

"I'm on my way up."

A little while later, Dylan walked into her office.

"Thank you for coming."

"What can I do for you, Savannah?" Dylan asked.

"Close the door, Dylan."

"Okay," he said nervously and closed the door.

"Have a seat." Once he was seated in one of the chairs in front of her desk, Savannah asked him for a favor. "I need access to the board of directors' cloud. Can you help me?"

"I could, but I could get fired for doing it."

"But you can?"

"Yes. I can. But like I said, I could get fired for doing it."

"I will protect you."

"Suppose you're gone."

"Then you'll have a job wherever I land."

"Okay." Dylan and Savannah switched places, and he gave her access to the board of directors' cloud account. "Anything in particular that you're looking for?"

"Internal memos."

"Dating back to how far?"

"To the last five years of Tia Richards's tenure."

"Done. I created a back door so you can access the information at your leisure. And yes, I do mean after I leave your office."

"Thank you, Dylan."

"You're welcome. Don't mention it to anybody."

"It will be our little secret," Savannah said as he left.

Savannah now had access to evidence that the financial condition of Intuitive Energy was prolonged by a long-standing, methodical, and imaginatively planned accounting scheme. The documents that she obtained were internal memos to the board of directors and select members of upper management, saying that Intuitive Energy used these uniquely purposed entities to mask substantial liabilities from Intuitive Energy's financial statements.

These entities made Intuitive Energy seem more profitable than it was. The deception created the misconception of billions of dollars in profit while it was actually losing money. The members of the board of directors at Intuitive Energy—Erica Horne, Riley Riviera, Elisha Carr, Safa Woodard, Lacey Ray, Ida Pennington, and the chairman of the board, Brodrick Fowler—all knew about the offshore accounts that were hiding losses for the company.

Since Brodrick Fowler was out of the country on business, at those times, it was Savannah who would be called upon to issue statements to the press or make appearances to calm investors and assure them that Intuitive Energy was doing well. Even though Intuitive Energy's stock price had decreased to $40 a share, investors still believed that Intuitive Energy's stock would rebound.

As the months rolled on, several financial analysts began to look carefully into the details of Intuitive Energy's publicly released financial statements. Intuitive Energy shocked investors when it announced that it was going to post a major third-quarter loss and planned to take a $1.2 billion reduction in shareholders.

And since the reported loss took place during Savannah's tenure as president, much of the blame for losses fell on her. In reality, the losses had been accumulated over several years. But that didn't matter.

Brodrick Fowler held a press conference to announce the loss. Although he didn't come right out and say it, the tone he took made it clear that Savannah's leadership was the cause of the loss.

"Believe me, Savannah, that was not my intention. I know, and more importantly, the board knows you are not responsible for the loss. It was accumulated over several years."

"That's how it looks down here," Savannah said.

"And nothing could be further from the truth," Brodrick may have assured, but Savannah wasn't buying a minute of it.

Savannah thought back to the days when he first hired her.

"'I knew I hired the right person,'" she said aloud. "He hired a fool, tailor-made to take the fall for years and years of deception to create the illusion of Intuitive Energy making a profit while the company was losing money."

What she should have done was resign right then, but she didn't, and if you asked Savannah why she didn't, she wouldn't be able to tell you.

Kiera came into Savannah's office and said that Brodrick Fowler called and asked Savannah to add a conference call to her schedule for tomorrow morning at ten.

"Did he say what the call will be about?"

"No. Sorry, he didn't. All I got was it's important."

The following morning at ten, Savannah logged in to participate in a conference call with Brodrick Fowler. On that call, Savannah was introduced to Jenson Cardenas, the new director of sales and marketing. Intuitive Energy had initiated Intuitive Energy Online. It was intended to be an Internet-based trading operation that promoted the company's aggressive investment strategy.

"I'd like you to mentor him, show him the ropes, you know, how we do things at Intuitive Energy."

"Not a problem, Brodrick," Savannah may have said, but she felt as if she had more than enough to do without having to play mentor for some new corporate asshole like him.

However, the following day, when Jenson Cardenas did come to her office, Savannah took one look at him and thought he might just be the sexiest man she'd ever met. But, when he began talking and trying to flirt with her, she thought he was an asshole, so she was not interested.

"He may be good for somebody. Just not me," Savannah told Ciara when she came to see about the actions that she could take to protect herself from what was going on at Intuitive Energy.

"The Supreme Court has identified four elements to prove insider trading: a lie or deception, a transgression of a fiduciary obligation, the use of secret information concerning a securities transaction, and willfulness by the defendant."

Savannah looked at Ciara as if she were speaking another language. "What does any of that even mean?"

"I think that a lie or deception is pretty broad, and I believe that's by design so they can use it for anything they deem appropriate. A transgression of a fiduciary obligation . . . fiduciary duty is the duty that arises from a relationship of trust."

"Such as?"

"Such as between an executive and their company. I think those last two are pretty self-explanatory. Don't you think?"

"I guess. I gotta tell you, now that all this is going on, I should have stayed in my quiet little job at BHV."

"Why don't you resign? Give Fowler two weeks' notice. Tell him it just isn't for you and move on. I would defend you, but I'd hate to see you go to jail for insider trading. Especially since you're not trading. Are you?"

"Oh, hell to the no."

"Good. Because the penalties are crazy."

"For example?"

"You can get as much as twenty years in prison. And you could be required to pay a fine of five million dollars."

"I don't have five million dollars, and I haven't traded any of the stock I received when they hired me."

"Good. If anything comes of this, that is going to work in your favor."

"At least there are some things working in my favor," Savannah said and stood up. "To the Four Seasons Hotel, to meet with the man Fowler wants me to speak with. That's where he's staying."

"I have to tell you, Savannah, I don't trust Mr. Brodrick Fowler."

"I don't either, Ciara. I don't either." Savannah paused and thought for a moment or two. "You know, when I first started there, I was so hopeful and excited about the opportunity. Me, a poor black girl from the projects, the president of a major energy company."

"I know. And I was so proud of you. My girl done made it to the big dance and she's running things."

"Yeah. That was me. Now it seems like Fowler hired me to be the fall guy," Savannah laughed. "I can't help thinking about my first day."

"What happened on your first day?"

"Duncan Anderson asked me, 'Why do you think they gave Tia Richards a golden parachute and they brought you in?'"

"Why?"

"He said that I was the cleanup woman. Now I'm the face of everything that goes on here."

"That's deep, Savannah."

"Tell me about it. I should have followed my first mind and walked out right then, but I thought he meant that I was there to clean up whatever mess Tia Richards made. But I had done a lot of research about her and the company. The press loved her."

"Why did she retire?"

"The usual. To spend more time with family."

"Everybody says that."

"Suppose everybody saw this coming, so they retire Tia Richards and bring me in to take the fall? Because with Brodrick being out of the country, it's me telling investors that everything is just peachy keen and they should keep their stock and buy more because the stock price is going to rebound."

"You should resign before it gets too deep over there."

"I have a contract. I am sure they will sue me if I resign before it expires."

"Bitch, please."

"What?"

"One of your besties is a lawyer. I'll take care of that for you."

"I know you will, but—"

"But nothing, Savannah. If you wanted to walk out of there right now, I'd have your back."

Savannah got up. "I need to go meet this guy."

Ciara got up and walked Savannah to the elevator. "Call me."

"I will," Savannah said, and she got on the elevator.

Chapter Fourteen

On Wednesday morning, Ciara got ready to leave her house for her trip to Saint Barts to review the records of Tobias and Leona Chandler. Other than these all being billable hours, Ciara had never been to Saint Barts, and it was one of the places that she'd always wanted to visit. In fact, she and Zack were talking about going, but, as usual, he had a case he was working on and couldn't get away.

When Ciara finished packing, she rolled her luggage to the door. She didn't know how much free time she was going to have, but there were a few things that she wanted to do while she was in Saint Barts. She'd heard about the shopping in Gustavia or St. Jean from Sharon Mason, so that was definitely on her agenda. Temperatures were usually somewhere between the low seventies and low nineties all year. Ciara planned to relax on one of the secluded beaches Saint Barts was famous for.

While she waited for the limousine to arrive, Ciara gave some thought to how these last two years with Zack had shaped her life around him, his needs, and what he wanted to do. They did the things that Zack wanted to do. They went to the places that Zack wanted to go. It was time for Ciara to start living her life on her own terms, and she was excited to explore this new chapter of her life.

When the limousine driver called, Ciara came down with her luggage. Once she was in the limousine, he put her luggage in the trunk and then drove Ciara to a private airfield where the Chandlers' private jet was waiting for the five-hour flight to Saint Barts.

Once the jet touched down, Ciara was escorted to the limousine, and she was driven to the Chandlers' ten-bedroom luxury beachfront Dutch colonial estate.

When Ciara arrived at the house, she was met by a man who introduced himself as Bill Blakey. As another man came and got her luggage out of the trunk, Bill escorted Ciara into the house.

"I'll show you to your room."

"Thank you."

"When you're ready, I will show you where you'll be working and give you a tour of the property. You are free to go anywhere on the grounds. The Chandlers' bedroom is the third level of the estate."

"I will conduct myself appropriately. I don't go places that I'm not invited."

Bill looked at Ciara and knew that she would be invited to the third level. They walked up the elegant glass staircase, which led to the upper levels.

"This is your room, Ms. Reynolds," Bill said, and he opened the double doors to the bedroom. "Let me know when you've settled in and I'll come get you."

"Thank you, Bill," Ciara said, and he closed the door.

Ciara looked around the spacious room. It had an area with a desk so she would be able to work in the room. She went into the en-suite bath, in which she saw fixtures that were marble and a soaking tub. She opened the French doors and went out onto the deck. She leaned over the rail and looked out at the view of the Caribbean Sea and the tranquil tropical garden below.

Once Ciara was settled into the room, she called Bill, and he showed her around the house. Their first stop was the kitchen, where she was introduced to Leila, the chef, and Luisa, her valet.

"It's a pleasure to meet you."

"Tonight, we're having blackened tuna steaks with mango salsa. However, I am at your disposal. Just let me know what you'd like to eat, and I will be more than happy to cook it for you."

"Looking forward to tasting the blackened tuna," Ciara said as Bill escorted her out of the kitchen.

He showed her the spacious living room, a media room, and a dazzling entertainment room. Then they went outside, where Bill showed her the gazebo and the tropical garden that she saw from her room. There was an Olympic-sized swimming pool as well as access to a semi-private beach.

They returned to the house, and Bill took Ciara to the office where she'd be working. Like everything else in the estate, the office, which was also a library, was huge.

"You'll find everything you need here. If there is something you need to find, please call and I will get what you need. Is there anything you need to get started?"

"No. Thank you, Bill. I'll be fine. I'm gonna run upstairs, get my laptop, and get started."

When Ciara returned to the office with her laptop, she got set up and began to look over the information that they had made available for her to review. At five o'clock, Bill came into the office and announced that dinner was served. He escorted Ciara to the dining room. She was surprised that there was only one place setting at the table.

"Are Mr. and Mrs. Chandler going to be joining me for dinner?" she asked as, along with the blackened tuna steaks with mango salsa with roasted lemon potatoes, Luisa served a lobster bisque entrée and a sliced tomato and cucumber salad.

"No. They will not be joining you this evening for dinner, Ms. Reynolds," Bill said.

"Are they here on the property?"

"Oh, yes. They simply won't be joining you for dinner this evening. I'm sure that Mr. and Mrs. Chandler will see you tomorrow," he informed.

"Okay. Because I already have a number of questions I'd like to ask."

"In the meantime, enjoy your meal. If you'd like to go off the property to experience the island, you simply need to call me, and I will arrange for the limousine to take you wherever you'd like to go."

"Thank you, Bill."

"As I said, enjoy your meal."

"Now that you mention it, Bill, I am going to take you up on that limousine."

"Just let me know when you're ready," Bill said and left Ciara alone to eat.

After dinner, Ciara dressed in a floral poppy draped minidress by A.L.C., and her driver took her to Nikki Beach Saint Barth, where she found a day-to-night beach party before ending up at Le Ti St Barth, which hosted a cabaret-style dinner theater and a dance club. Ciara thoroughly enjoyed the cabaret show, and then she danced the night away. It was almost four in the morning when the limousine dropped her off at the Chandlers' estate.

However, despite having a mild hangover, Ciara was up at nine and wandered into the kitchen.

"Good morning, Ms. Reynolds."

"Good morning, Luisa."

"Did you enjoy yourself last night?" Luisa asked.

"I really did." Ciara sat down at the table. "Is there any coffee?"

"Yes, we have coffee. Would you like arabica or robusta beans?"

"I didn't know there was a difference."

"Neither did I." Ciara laughed with Luisa. "How do you take it?"

"With sugar and lots of cream, please."

"Good morning, Ms. Reynolds," Leila said when she came into the kitchen.

"Morning," Ciara sang.

"How did you sleep?"

"Not enough."

"What can I make for you this morning?"

"Just some eggs. Maybe a little bacon."

"How do you want your eggs?"

"Any way you like is fine."

Luisa giggled, and then she covered her mouth.

"What?" Ciara asked. "Did I say something wrong?"

"No, Ms. Reynolds, you didn't say anything wrong. It's just that most of our guests, once you tell them that I will cook their food any way they like, tend to want something elaborate. But not you, Ms. Reynolds. 'Any way you like is fine,'" Leila giggled. "It's just refreshing to know that there are still people like you in the world."

"Thank you. I guess," Ciara giggled as Luisa brought her coffee.

"I brewed arabica beans and added lots of caramel latte creamer."

"Thank you," Ciara said and took a sip. "This is excellent."

"I am going to make you a shrimp and feta cheese omelet, Ms. Reynolds. Would that be acceptable? Or would you prefer to have some bacon? I do have some center-cut bacon if that's what you'd like."

"No, Leila. The shrimp and feta cheese omelet will be fine. Thank you." Ciara stood up. "Could you bring that to my room when it's ready, please?"

"I would be happy to, Ms. Reynolds," Luisa said as Ciara drifted out of the kitchen.

After a quick stop in the office to pick up some of the files she needed, Ciara headed back to her room. Once she put her materials down on the desk, Ciara opened the French doors to let the sun and warm Caribbean breeze into the room.

Then, since she was still a little hungover, she lay across the bed and closed her eyes. When Luisa brought breakfast, Ciara ate the shrimp and feta cheese omelet Leila prepared for her. It was delicious. After breakfast, Ciara got back in bed and slept until after one in the afternoon.

When she woke up, Ciara got back to work reviewing the Chandlers' legal and business records. She took a break for dinner, and thinking it was something elaborate, Ciara asked Leila to make her filet mignon with lobster thermidor.

It wasn't elaborate.

"Eight- or ten-ounce filet mignon?"

"Eight, thank you," Ciara said, a little disappointed that her dinner choice didn't move the elaborate needle.

After dinner, Ciara went back to work, and other than getting up to stretch her legs and stand out on the deck, she worked until almost eleven o'clock. She did think about changing clothes and calling for the limousine.

I see what Savannah loves about it.

But she quickly dismissed the thought.

What surprised her was that she hadn't seen either of her hosts. Although Bill said they were on the property, Ciara hadn't seen either of them. Not that she minded. Not seeing them at all was a whole lot better than the client hovering over her or interrupting to ask stupid questions, so Ciara wasn't complaining.

The following day was just about the same. Ciara had cranberry-orange pancakes for breakfast and worked by the pool. After a light lunch of slow-cooked Mediterranean lentil soup and a turkey pesto toasterdilla, she went into the office and worked there for the rest of the day. In the time she had been there, Ciara had completed her review of the Chandlers' legal and business records. She felt knowledgeable enough to take over representing them as their attorney. Therefore, her plan for the weekend was to do some shopping and spend some time relaxing in the spot on the beach she'd been eyeing since she first stepped out on the balcony.

After Luisa served her another elaborate breakfast of German apple pancakes and strawberry-filled red velvet crepes, Ciara called for the limousine and went shopping. When she returned, she put on the multicolor Valentino Garavani bikini she had just bought and headed for her secluded spot under a tree on the beach. Since she had a few notes she wanted to update, Ciara took her laptop to the beach with her. She was just about to note her final conclusion when Ciara saw a woman jogging down the beach. She hadn't seen many people on the beach since she'd been there, so it caught her eye. Ciara was looking at her laptop's screen when the woman abruptly stopped in front of her.

"Ciara?"

When she looked up and took off her sunglasses, Ciara saw that it was Leona Chandler. She was wearing a tight-fitting white Stefano Ricci jogging suit that hugged each of her curves.

"Good afternoon, Mrs. Chandler."

"Good afternoon. How long have you been here?"

"I arrived on Wednesday afternoon."

"Wednesday? Why wasn't I told?"

"I don't know why you weren't told."

Leona Chandler wasn't told that Ciara was on the property on the orders of Tobias Chandler. He knew that Leona had her own agenda in mind for Ciara, and he wanted her to get her work done without Leona hovering over her.

"Have you spoken with Tobias?"

"No, I haven't. The only people I've met since I've been here are Leila, Luisa, and Bill, and I haven't seen him since Wednesday evening." Ciara smiled because they'd been a bright spot on this trip.

Leona smiled for the first time. "Have Leila and Luisa taken good care of you?"

"Yes, they have. They've been a joy."

"Well, since you've been here since Wednesday, what have you been doing?"

"I've completed my review and would like to present my findings and make certain recommendations to strengthen your legal and business positions."

"I will make sure that Tobias and I are available sometime this afternoon. When are you leaving for Houston?"

"I had planned to fly back tomorrow."

"I see," Leona said, thought for a second or two, and then looked at Ciara. "Enjoy the beach, and I will see you at the house," she said and continued her run down the beach.

When Ciara returned to the estate, Bill told her that Mr. Chandler would be available that afternoon at five, and Leona wanted to speak with her by the pool. When Ciara got out to the pool, Leona was sunbathing naked.

That explains the lack of tan lines, Ciara thought as she approached. *What do you say to a naked woman? And an extremely attractive one at that?*

"Hello, Mrs. Chandler. You asked to see me."

"Yes. Please have a seat." Ciara took a seat in the chair next to Leona, trying but not succeeding in looking at her body. Therefore, Ciara focused her gaze on the multicolored cocktail Leona was sipping. "I wanted to let you know that Tobias and I will be available to meet with you this afternoon at five, if that's acceptable for you?"

"Yes. Bill had already informed me that was when Tobias wanted to meet." Ciara, hoping that was all Leona wanted, started to get up and go to her room until it was time to meet.

"So." Leona sat up and looked at Ciara. The way her full breasts swung caused Ciara to take a breath. "You find yourself surprisingly free until then. What would you like to do?" she asked and took a sip of her cocktail.

"I really didn't have anything planned. So, I was going to my room until it was time to meet."

Since she was still trying to focus on the glass instead of the way Leona's breasts moved when she breathed, Ciara asked about the cocktail, which was red at the bottom of the glass and green on top.

"If you don't mind me asking, what is that you're drinking?"

"I was wondering when you were going to ask. I noticed you've been looking at it." Leona smiled. "This is a Lick My Pussy Shot," she giggled, and her breasts jiggled. "It's a super dirty name, but it is so delicious. Would you like to try one?"

"I would love to."

Leona reached over and pressed a button on the table next to her. A minute later, Luisa came out to the pool.

"Bring two more Lick My Pussy Shots, please."

"Right away, Mrs. Chandler."

"What's in it?" Ciara asked, because what do you talk about with a naked woman? One whose nipples were getting harder the longer Ciara sat there.

"The recipe calls for coconut rum, but I have Luisa make mine with coconut and 151 rum. And it has melon liqueur, pineapple juice, and grenadine." Leona paused and once again looked Ciara directly into her eyes. "Does my being naked make you uncomfortable?"

"Not at all," Ciara said quickly. More because uncomfortable wasn't the word for what it was making her. "This is your house. You can sunbathe any way, any time you want."

"Good. I hate tan lines," Leona said as Luisa returned with two Lick My Pussy Shots for the ladies. Leona sipped hers.

"I mean, it's not like your being naked is you trying to seduce me," Ciara giggled not so innocently and sipped her Lick My Pussy Shot.

"Oh, I am very much trying to seduce you, Ciara. I was just taking my time because that makes the seduction so much more delicious when you don't rush. Don't you agree?"

"There is something to be said for the slow game."

Ciara wondered if she was going to comment on Leona's stated intention to seduce her or let it go without comment because she was all right with being seduced. She wasn't sure, at least not yet. *How bi-curious are you?* she wondered.

It was then that Tobias passed through the pool area with Bill.

"Tobias!" Leona called to him and waved for him to join them.

After saying a few words to Bill, Tobias came and sat down by the pool with his wife and Ciara.

"Good afternoon, Ms. Reynolds. Leona tells me that you've completed your work for us and have findings to present, and you have certain recommendations in mind to strengthen our legal and business positions."

"Yes, sir. I am excited to share those with you when you're available."

"I have time now if you're ready." Tobias relaxed on the chair next to Ciara. "Let's do it now."

For the next two hours, during which Leona neither paid attention nor put on clothes, Ciara explained her observations of their legal position, which was strong, and then she made what Ciara saw as action items that would not only strengthen their position but make them considerable money. Tobias was pleased with the presentation. He thought that Ciara Reynolds was a much better attorney than Sharon Mason, and she was much sexier.

Maybe her husband finding out what his wife was really doing down here so often was actually a good thing, he thought.

"That was excellent, Ms. Reynolds," Tobias said, and since he was thinking it, he told her, "You are a much better attorney than Ms. Mason."

"Well, thank you. That is very kind of you to say."

"I can only say it because I know it to be true," he said as Bill, along with Leila and Luisa, wheeled out a roasted pig that Leila had prepared for dinner. They had dinner that evening at the gazebo. Leona did not put on clothes while they ate. After dinner, Tobias excused himself, promising to join them later.

Leona, on the other hand, had other ideas.

Chapter Fifteen

Thalia bent over on the bed, and he entered her slowly. She began moaning, squirming, and winding her hips.

"Ooooooh!" Thalia screamed, savoring the sensation of having every inch of him inside her warmth. Griffin grabbed Thalia by the shoulders and thrust himself farther inside. "Oh, yes!"

Thalia collapsed on the bed, and he lay down next to her. She quickly got on top and rode him slowly. He was so deep inside her that her body trembled again.

That was when Griffin's cell began ringing. Thalia didn't care. She glanced at the clock next to the bed. *Maybe it's his wife calling, or it might be some other woman who wants to get what I'm getting.* Thalia could tell by the way he was holding on to her hips and pushing himself inside her that he had no intention of answering it.

Thalia began to move her hips from side to side and was in ecstasy as he sucked her nipples while she moved up and down on his erection. She sat up and placed her hands on his legs and then her feet on the bed. He arched his back and pushed himself as deep and as hard into her as he could.

Once again, the love they made together was off the chain. And, as they did whenever they got together, Griffin grabbed his bag and rushed to the shower. While Griffin showered, Thalia lay in bed thinking about what she was doing after years of accusing Cedric of cheating on her and not liking how it felt.

Now, she was the cheater.

And you know what? It feels so good.

And it wasn't just the sex that was good. And it was. Griffin brought it hard, long, and consistently with each and every stroke. It was being pursued that Thalia was getting into. There were four men pursuing her. Two of them, Griffin and Aston, she'd met and had sex with. Each time Thalia thought about that night in the car with Aston, she felt it deep in her core, and it caused her body to shatter.

When she heard the shower go off, Thalia decided she was going to have some fun. And besides, becoming a cheater had made her a little on the insatiable side. And she loved it. She got on her knees and knelt on the bed. Therefore, when Griffin came out of the bathroom, dressed and ready to go, Thalia's round ass and swollen lips would be the first things he saw.

"Damn." Griffin stopped in his tracks. "That is so unfair."

"Whoever said fuckin' was fair?"

"Nobody," he said, stroking his length until it got hard again. Griffin looked at his watch. "Fuck it. She's gonna be mad anyway," he said and unbuckled his pants. He entered her quickly and began pumping as hard and as fast as he could.

"Get it!" Thalia shouted over and over until he came hard inside her.

Griffin collapsed on her back and held on. Once Griffin had composed himself, he pulled out of Thalia.

"That was so unfair of you," he said and rushed back to the bathroom.

"Whoever said fuckin' was fair?"

This time, he just took a quick wash off instead of getting back into the shower, and Griffin came rushing out of the bathroom. He leaned over and kissed Thalia and was out of the room.

Since she wasn't in a hurry, Thalia got out of bed and took a long shower. As the water beat on her body, she laughed when she thought about the look on his face when he came out of the bathroom. She knew that it was his wife who called while she was riding hard. She'd heard him talking to her while he was in the bathroom before he turned on the shower.

"I'm at the gym. About to jump in the shower and head home," she'd heard him say.

Thalia thought about the times when Cedric told her that very same thing. Therefore, when she heard the shower come on and he rushed her off the phone, Thalia thought nothing of it. Of course, Cedric being Cedric, there was always the suspicion that he was actually with another woman.

"Or a man," she giggled and thought about her friend. "Poor Ciara," Thalia said, wondering that if Cedric were gay, would she know it? She thought she would be able to; however, Ciara had been with him for two years, and she had no clue.

"Probably not. In the closet is in the closet, I guess," she said aloud and turned off the water.

Thalia got dressed and headed home. When she turned on her street and hit the button for the garage door, she was once again surprised to see Cedric's SUV. In her absence, he had once again gotten a call from his daughter, and he came to pick them up from the neighbor's house.

"Hi, Mommy!" Sylvie shouted and bit another bite of her slice of pizza.

"How's everybody?" Thalia said to the four of them seated around the table.

"Where have you been?" Cedric asked from his seat at the head of the kitchen table.

"I was at Jade Emperor, having dinner with Stephanie Crawford with Quanta Leap."

It was what he always did when she would ask that same question. She figured out that when he used that excuse, he had already closed the client. Therefore, she did the same. Stephanie Crawford had signed the contract virtually over a month ago and would be coming to the office later that week. It was one of his excuses, and now it was hers.

Cedric took another bite of his slice. "How'd it go?"

"Great!" Thalia sat down at the table and got a slice of pizza. "She'll be in the office to see me on Thursday."

Which just happened to be the day that Cedric liked to make cold calls to existing clients. Therefore, he wouldn't be in the office, and if he were to come there, Thalia would deal with that once it happened.

Later that night, after they had sex and Cedric went to sleep, Thalia got out of bed and went into the living room. She got her personal laptop and went online to Black People Come Together. She and Griffin decided not to leave text messages on their phones. Griffin's wife had a habit of checking and reading his messages.

"I have to pass random phone checks," Griffin told Thalia.

"Phone checks? What are phone checks?"

"You don't check your husband's phone?"

"No."

"Wow. I gotta run a program called iShredder."

"Never heard of it. What does it do?"

"They use something called data shredding. It overwrites the data multiple times, and it makes it hard to recover," Griffin said, and Thalia wondered if Cedric had one on his phone just in case one day Thalia asked for his phone.

Maybe I should get one, she thought and closed her laptop, went back in the room, and got in bed with Cedric.

The following morning, Thalia got dressed in a Lela Rose bolero jacket, a midi dress, and Stuart Weitzman slingback pumps.

"Where are you going?" Cedric asked.

"I'm working off-site this week. Doing an internal audit of Dr. Michael Wilkerson's practice. He is up for his second Medicare review for some type of fraud. He says he doesn't know where the fraud is coming from, so hopefully I can tell him where and, more importantly, who is causing the issue."

"In my experience, it's always the office manager. These doctors open these offices to practice medicine but don't know the first thing about running a business. So, what do they do?"

"They hire somebody to run the office."

"And they're the ones who, in my experience, rob them blind."

"I'll be on the lookout for that."

That morning, Thalia and her audit team entered the practice of Dr. Michael and Dr. Aurora Wilkerson. They received notice from Medicaid that there were once again potentially false claims submitted and noted suspicious billing patterns from the practice.

Her team would analyze documents and records, observing actions or processes inside the organization using analytical techniques, which entailed examining both financial and non-financial data, to find patterns, irregularities, or discrepancies. Thalia would conduct the inquiries of the staff personally. She interviewed and obtained written statements from the doctors, management, and staff to clarify differences or grasp procedures that may have caused errors in reporting.

Thalia was waiting in Dr. Michael Wilkerson's office so she could get started conducting interviews. However, she was not prepared for her reaction when he walked into the room.

"Mrs. Blackburn. Good morning," he said and shook her hand. His hand was warm.

"Good morning, Dr. Wilkerson." *My God,* she thought, because he had taken her breath away. *He is so fine.*

"Sorry to keep you waiting," he said, and the dreadlocks that hung by his shoulders swung when he sat down behind his desk. His auburn skin seemed as if it was glistening, and his light eyes were focused solely on her. She couldn't look away even if she wanted to.

"Not a problem," Thalia was barely able to get out. "Will your wife be joining us?"

"Ex-wife. We divorced, and she remarried." The doctor smiled, and Thalia got a little wetter. "She is now Dr. Aurora Wilkerson Scott."

He reached for a picture frame on the desk and then turned it so Thalia could see it.

"That's them on their wedding day," Dr. Wilkerson said of the picture of two women in white wedding dresses. "And no. She's with a patient right now. But she promised to make time for you later."

"Very good."

"As I explained to your assistant, Medicare has flagged what they say are potentially false claims being submitted, and they've noted some of what they say are suspicious billing patterns coming from this office. I need to know, and I'm hoping you and your team could tell me, what's going on, who is doing it, put a stop to it, and recommend ways to keep it from happening again."

"I believe that we can help you get to the bottom of it and be able to move forward with Medicare off your back."

"That's all I could ask for." Dr. Wilkerson stood up. "You are welcome to use my office to conduct your investigation."

"Thank you, Dr. Wilkerson."

He stopped on the way to the door. "Michael."

She smiled. "Thalia."

"You look very nice in that outfit," Michael flirted.

"Thank you."

"I'll check in with you later. See how things are going," he said, looking into her eyes.

"That will be fine," Thalia said, and she closed the door behind him.

She went and sat down behind his desk. She inhaled and breathed in the scent of him and prepared to get to work.

By one forty-one that afternoon, Thalia had spoken with half of the staff at the practice of Michael and Aurora Wilkerson. There was a knock at the door.

"Come in," Thalia said, and Michael walked into the office.

"How's it going?"

"It's going fairly well. I've spoken to half of the people I intend to."

"And?"

"And I'll share my observations with you when our review is complete."

"Not even a hint?" he said playfully and sat down.

"It wouldn't be a comprehensive answer because I don't have all the information I'd need to say with any certainty."

"Okay, be like that. I came to see if you were hungry."

"Starving. I didn't eat breakfast this morning, and I've been drinking coffee and terrorizing your doughnuts until they were gone."

Michael laughed. "That is what they're for. But I wanted to know if you wanted to join me for lunch."

"That would be nice."

"Great. Do you like Chinese food?"

"I love Chinese food."

"Awesome. There's a Chinese food buffet in the plaza. We could walk down there and either grab something and bring it back, or we could sit down and eat."

Thalia stood up. "I think I'd rather sit down and eat." *So I can look into those pretty eyes.* "I need a change of scenery for a minute."

So, Thalia and Michael left the office and walked down to the Chinese food buffet. After they finished eating, they stayed in the restaurant for several more hours talking, and each found the other fascinating. There was an energy flowing between them that each one recognized almost immediately. It was four thirty-eight when Thalia and Michael returned to the practice.

Consequently, when Thalia returned to her office, Cedric had heard about the long lunch break with Michael, and he was livid.

"What's up with you and the three-hour lunch?" Cedric demanded to know.

His tone of voice and the angry look on his face caught Thalia off guard. "We were talking about the audit."

"For three hours?" Cedric got up and closed his office door. "Are you cheatin' on me, Thalia?"

She laughed. Stopped. Looked at Cedric and started laughing again.

"Cheating? Is that what you're asking me?" She shook her head. "I just met the man this morning. So, what do you think? I just went to a nearby hotel for a quick fuck?"

Although that does sound good.

"Not with him. I ain't stupid. I know you just met that man. But you're cheatin' on me with somebody. I can feel it."

"If anybody can feel cheating, it's you."

"What's that supposed to mean?"

"It means that you're a cheater who has been cheating on me for years."

"I never cheated on you."

Thalia laughed. "What about Nora Peck?"

"That was a simple misunderstanding."

"Right. I understand you fucked her. And then there was Keisha Potter."

"She was working late, and that's why people would always see her coming out of my office at night."

"Every night? Nigga, please. I know what it's like to get fucked on this desk," Thalia said, tapping on the edge of the desk.

Cedric smiled as he thought back to that day. "We had to christen it, didn't we?"

"Yes. I was the first of many."

"Whatever."

"What about Tristan Ramos? Was she a misunderstanding too?"

"It wasn't a misunderstanding, but there was nothing between me and that woman."

"Whatever, Cedric. You're a cheater. You've cheated on me for years. I just never have seen the need to confront you about it for the sake of peace in my home." Thalia opened the door to Cedric's office.

"Where are you going?"

Thalia looked Cedric directly in the eyes. "I'm going to meet with a client," she lied with a straight face. "I'll be home around ten," she said and closed the door.

Thalia went to her office and took her laptop from the bag. She went online and left a message for Griffin, telling him that she was free and asking if he wanted to get together. It had been thirty minutes, and she hadn't gotten a response.

"What now?" she asked herself.

Now that she'd made a big deal of saying she'd be home at ten, Thalia decided to take a chance that the energy she felt wasn't all on her side.

"Dr. Michael Wilkerson."

"Hello, Michael. It's Thalia Blackburn."

"Yes, Thalia. This is an unexpected but pleasant surprise."

"I am never this forward, but would you like to go out with me tonight?"

"I would love that," he said without a second of hesitation. "We just ate, so what would you like to do?"

We could go to that hotel I saw across the street from your office, and you should fuck me silly. Thalia laughed. "I have no idea. I'm making this up as I go along."

"Tell you what. Why don't we go see a movie? And if we get hungry, there's always popcorn and hot dogs."

"Sounds good."

So, Thalia met Michael at the theater, and they watched and enjoyed a romantic comedy called *Holding on to Sheila*. After the movie was over, Thalia went and had a drink at a bar on the way to her house and stayed there until it was time. She walked in the door, as promised, at exactly ten o'clock. When she got home, Cedric was on the phone with whoever he was supposed to be with that night, so he didn't hear Thalia come in. She was showered and in bed when he came into their bedroom.

"How long have you been here?" Cedric asked as he got undressed.

"Since ten."

"I'm not even gonna bother to ask you where you've been," Cedric said, and once he was naked, he got in bed with Thalia.

"Good. Because I wasn't gonna bother to answer you," Thalia said, and she prepared to receive him.

"Is this how it's gonna be from now on?" Cedric asked, and he entered Thalia.

"Yes."

Chapter Sixteen

When Ciara arrived at Euphoria Elixirs, she looked around for Savannah and Thalia. She didn't see them, so she went ahead and found a booth. They were there to meet FBI Agent Jared Clarke. They met two years ago when she needed information for a case that she was defending, which involved the FBI. He came to her office, and she got the information she needed. He asked her if she wanted to go have dinner or get a drink. However, that was the day after Zack proposed, so she gladly showed him her ring.

As she waited, a woman with long, straight black hair walked out of the bar who reminded her of Leona Chandler. It caused her to think about that Saturday night at the estate in Saint Barts. Thoughts of those lips sucking and nibbling everywhere Ciara wanted made her clit swell between her thighs, so she crossed her legs.

Maybe it was the number of Lick My Pussy Shots she drank. She and Leona had been sipping cocktails from late afternoon through and after dinner. It helped melt away that last wall of defense. And since Ciara was already curious about what it would be like, it was easy for Leona to talk her out of her bikini and get in the Jacuzzi.

"Bring two more Lick My Pussy Shots to the Jacuzzi."

This was the slow seduction that Leona said was so much sweeter. That was Ciara's opportunity to shut it down. She should have said something like, "I'm sorry if I've given you the wrong impression. I am here to be your attorney and nothing more."

But she didn't. Ciara reinforced it. "There is something to be said for the slow game."

Now, slow game, or slow seduction, when Leona leaned in and kissed Ciara's lips gently, teasing her with soft, swift pecks, it had Ciara swirling with lust for her. She closed her eyes and leaned back as Leona leaned into her neck. She began kissing and suckling Ciara in spots, and her breasts were in the palms of Leona's hands.

Ciara watched Leona move between her thighs. She slapped one of her breasts and then pushed them together. Leona squeezed her hard nipples together and began to lick and suck them. She took each nipple into her warm mouth, sucking both as if Ciara's nipples were the sweetest things her mouth had ever tasted. Ciara closed her eyes as Leona's lips and tongue switched between them both, lingering to taste the pebbled flesh around each nipple. One by one, back and forth.

"Sit up here on the edge."

Leona helped Ciara out of the Jacuzzi, and once she was sitting on the edge, her lips traveled down Ciara's stomach. It wasn't long before Ciara felt her tongue circling around her already swollen bud. Leona gently eased her thighs apart and had Ciara's toes curling as she used her tongue to make circles around her Brazilian-waxed clit. She parted her lips with her tongue and then used that wet tongue to flick back and forth across Ciara's clit.

With her legs in the air, Ciara held her head in place with one hand and squeezed her nipple with the other as Leona eased two fingers in and out of her. Ciara felt a wave rush over her entire body.

"Oh, shittt!"

"There she is," Ciara heard Thalia say. She looked up and saw them coming toward the table.

"I see her," Savannah said, and they went to the table.

Ciara forced thoughts of Leona's lips to the back of her mind and waved to her friends.

"How long have you been here?" Savannah asked when she slid into the booth.

"I just got here."

"Well," Savannah began, "thank you for setting this up. Since I received that email, this has been the only thing I've been focused on. Getting to this conversation."

"You know I'm glad to help. Whatever I can do."

"Well, I know I appreciate both of you."

"I'm just here for moral support," Thalia said.

"Not true. You advised me early on that Intuitive Energy's accounting method was, at best, unconventional. Otherwise, I wouldn't have known," Savannah said. "And there is value in that."

The server came to the table to take drink orders.

"To be honest with you, Savannah," Ciara said once their server had gone to get their drinks, "I think that's why they hired you. They were counting on you not knowing that their accounting practices opened the door to the fraud they are committing."

"I think she's right," Thalia said.

"Don't think I haven't thought the same thing. Especially after all this came my way. I assumed that they hired me to clean up the mess, but I'm perfectly positioned to be the fall guy. Like Duncan said, they hired me to be the face of the company as it crashes and burns. I'll be lucky if I stay out of jail."

"I'm not going to let that happen, Savannah. This is the first step to keeping you out of jail."

"Snitch," Savannah laughed.

"Whistleblower is the accepted term for what you're doing," Thalia pointed out as their server returned with the drinks.

"Call it what you want. Fact is, I'm here to start snitching about everything I know, heard, or suspected at Initiative."

"And I'm here to protect you," Ciara said as FBI Agent Jared Clarke arrived at Euphoria Elixirs. "Here he comes now." Ciara waved. "I don't remember him being that fine. Probably because my head was so far up Zack's gay ass."

"Good evening, ladies," Jared said. "I'm FBI Agent Jared Clarke."

"I know who you are," Ciara said.

"Can I sit?"

"Of course," Thalia said, smiling because she thought Jared Clarke was fine too. She extended her hand. "Thalia Blackburn. I'm her accounting adviser."

"Pleasure to meet you." Jared turned to Savannah. "And that makes you Savannah Ayers."

"Guilty as charged," Savannah said with her hand extended. "It's a pleasure to meet you."

"Likewise," Jared said and looked at the cocktails on the table. He stood up. "I'm going to get a drink from the bar. We can get started when I get back."

"Sounds good," Savannah said, and the three of them watched as Jared walked away from the table and headed for the bar. "You didn't say he was that sexy."

"That's because I don't remember him being that fine," Ciara said.

"Well, he is," Thalia added.

When Jared returned to the table, he said, "So, Savannah, tell me what's going on at Intuitive Energy."

"It begins with their use of mark-to-market accounting as a valuation method."

"I advised her that although using mark-to-market accounting as their valuation method was unconventional, the Financial Accounting Standards Board provides guidelines for mark-to-market under generally accepted accounting principles."

"What, in your opinion, do you allege violates the generally accepted accounting principles?"

At that point, Savannah began to detail for Agent Clarke all that she had noted during her time at the helm of Intuitive Energy. She showed him the email from Marilyn Proctor, as well as the board of directors' internal memorandums, which laid out, in a fair amount of detail, the fraudulent activities and to still push the stock.

"As I said to the lovely Ciara Reynolds, this is just an informal discussion. But I think there is more than enough here for you to speak with someone from the U.S. Securities and Exchange Commission. They're the ones who will open the investigation, and if massive fraud exists, and I believe it does, the FBI may get involved."

"Will you make the referral?" Savannah asked.

"Yes. In the form of an official referral to the U.S. Securities and Exchange Commission."

"Thank you, Jared," Savannah said, and he chuckled.

"Don't thank me yet, Savannah. They are about to take you through the wringer. But you have a good support team here." He looked at Ciara. "I'm sure they'll be there every step of the way."

Thalia held Savannah's hand. "You know I got your back."

Ciara was still looking into Jared's eyes, and he was all up in hers. "I'll be the one sitting next to you while they try to take you through the wringer."

"Thank all of you."

When their server returned to the table to see if anybody wanted another drink or needed to see a menu,

Jared ordered another drink, and he wanted to see a menu. It was when he encouraged Ciara to join him for a drink and dinner that Savannah and Thalia knew it was their cue to leave.

"I'm gonna shove up," Thalia said. "I need to get home and feed my young'uns."

"I'm going to get out of here too," Savannah said without giving a reason for her departure. She slid out of the booth, as did Thalia. "Jared, it was nice meeting you. I'm sure I'll see you again as the process continues."

Jared stood up, and he shook hands with Savannah and then with Thalia. "I'm sure I will. It was my pleasure meeting you ladies."

"Good night," Thalia said.

"Call me," Savannah said to Ciara, and she and Thalia left Euphoria Elixirs.

"So," Ciara said. "What are you going to order?"

"The Bourbon Street steak sounds good. What about you?"

"I wasn't planning to stay for dinner, but—"

"I'm not keeping you from your fiancé, am I?"

"No." Then Ciara thought about it. "That's right. I got engaged the night before I met you." Ciara reached for the menu. "I ended my engagement with him."

"I'm sorry. Do you mind if I ask why so I don't make the same mistake and mess up my chance with you, beautiful Ciara?"

"I doubt it. But let me ask you now so it won't become an issue for me and traumatize me all over again. Are you gay?"

"Excuse me?"

"Do you like to fuck other men in the ass?"

Jared's face immediately became a twisted mass of hell the fuck no. "No!" he all but shouted.

"Then I think you're on safe ground."

"I'm sorry that happened to you."

"Trust and believe that I am too."

Feeling it was best to move on at that point, Jared signaled for their server. When she arrived, he told her what he wanted to eat.

"What about you, honey?"

"I'll have the blackened Cajun salmon."

The server took the menus, promised to have their order out as soon as possible, and left the table.

"Now, let's talk about you not wanting to ruin your chances." Ciara picked up and sipped her drink. "Chances of what?"

"Of getting to know you, of course," Jared said and leaned forward. "I don't know if you know it or not . . ." Jared paused. "Maybe you don't since your man was gay," he chuckled. "How did you put it? Liked fucking other men in the ass."

Ciara smiled and laughed. "Watch it. I can talk about my butt-fucking ex but not you."

"Sorry. Anyway, you are a beautiful woman, Ciara Reynolds, so yes, I would love to take this beyond dinner tonight, beautiful Ciara, and see if we can develop some type of relationship."

"I think I'd like to see how this meal goes before I commit to anything, but I gotta say, so far, you are off to a good start."

"Good. Because I want to see you again, beautiful Ciara."

"You keep calling me beautiful Ciara and it will go a long way toward making that a reality."

"I will. Especially since you haven't shut me down because I got right to my intended purpose."

"I happen to like that quality in a man."

Jared wanted to say something like, "How would you know? You didn't have a man," but he went with, "I got no problem telling you what I want. And yes, beautiful Ciara, I want you."

"As I said, let's see how this meal goes before we start to talk relationship. But I'll tell you that you're off to a good start tonight."

"Good to know," Jared said as their server returned to the table with that evening's meal. At the conclusion of that meal, Jared walked her to her car and said good night to Ciara.

If she wanted to be honest, Ciara would have to admit that she wanted to take him home with her or go to his place or a nearby hotel because, truth be told, it was Ciara who wanted to get fucked in her ass. And on top of that, Ciara still had thoughts of sex with Leona Chandler on her mind.

Ciara was well aware that Zack had turned her into a little freak, and if she allowed it, Leona would be more than happy to turn Ciara out as she had Sharon Mason. She fell in love with Leona, and that had her running down to Saint Barts every chance she got.

"That will not be me, I promise you that."

Although Ciara had satisfied her curiosity and decided she wanted to be with men, she had tasted the fruit.

Ciara called Rahim to come over to her house. He was more than happy to fill the role of fuck buddy in Ciara's life, and she was happy to be able to call on him to fuck her when she wanted to get fucked.

Chapter Seventeen

"You know I could show you better than I could tell you," Thalia said and dropped to her knees. She unbuckled his belt, unzipped his pants, and pulled out his long, rock-hard length. Thalia admired it before lowering her head to it.

Thalia gazed up at him as she allowed her tongue to slither across the head. The look on Griffin's face never softened. So, Thalia took the entire head into her mouth. She closed her eyes as if she were savoring her favorite flavor. Griffin relaxed a bit and eased back onto the bed. She slurped and sucked, wetting his head more and more. She opened her eyes and looked at Griffin. When she thought he was ready, she deep throated him and squeezed her jaws, tightening her grip around him. Griffin grabbed a fistful of her hair and began to guide her head closer and closer into his lap.

Thalia sucked harder. She could feel his hips moving in sync with her own motions. She wanted to keep him in that position for as long as possible, but she felt the floodgates release between her own thighs. Thalia moved faster, and Griffin's breathing was off the chart. He was all hot and bothered, just the way Thalia wanted him. Before he could move another inch, she dug in her purse and pulled out a black and gold wrapper.

Griffin looked up at her from his spot on the bed. His breathing had returned to normal. Thalia snatched the wrapper open and used one hand to slip the condom on his throbbing erection. Before Griffin could make another move, she straddled him. She didn't do it slow or easy. She slid right onto him and began to ride him unmercifully.

As the sounds of her flesh meeting his flesh filled the room, Thalia locked her arms around Griffin's neck and used her hips to move up and down on his massive rod. He guided her by the hips and kept up with her vigor.

Suddenly, Griffin grabbed both of her breasts, squeezed them together, and brought her hard nipples into his mouth. He sucked and lathered them. Then abruptly, Griffin stopped, held her shoulders tightly, and thrust his hips into her midsection. Thalia's eyes widened, and with her mouth agape, she squeezed her walls tighter. However, Griffin shoved her up and off his still throbbing dick.

Griffin stretched her out face down over the arm of the bed, and before she could protest any longer, he slammed himself into her from behind. She released a gut-wrenching scream and dug her fingernails into the mattress.

"Oh, yes, Griffin! Right there! Right there, baby!" she cried as Griffin hammered away. "Oh, Griffin," she moaned. "Yes, Griffin, yessss, yes!"

Once Thalia got through screaming his name, Griffin grabbed his bag, went into the bathroom, and took a shower. When he came out of the bathroom, Thalia was lying across the bed.

He was actually looking forward to coming out of the bathroom and seeing Thalia's pretty ass in the air waiting for him to break her off some. However, when he came out of the bathroom, she wasn't looking for any dick. She was simply lying across the bed.

As Griffin got dressed to leave, Thalia got out of bed and walked over to him.

"I'm gonna get in the shower and get out of here too," she said and kissed him on the cheek. "You have a good night with wifey," she taunted on her way to the shower.

"I might if she were throwing pussy like you do," he said and put on his pants.

"Ain't nobody throwing pussy like I do." Thalia closed the bathroom door, and once Griffin was dressed, he left the room and went home to wifey.

When Thalia came out of the bathroom, as expected, Griffin was long gone. She expected no less. She looked at the time. He said that he needed to be home by seven o'clock, and it was seven thirty.

"He'll be all right," Thalia said as she got dressed, and once she was dressed, she went to pick up the children from where she had left them.

And once again, she turned into her driveway, opened the garage door, and found Cedric's SUV parked in his parking space. Thalia had to laugh because if she knew that the way to get her cheating husband to come home was to start cheating herself, she would've done it a long time ago. Once again, he had gotten a call from his daughter.

"I hate that woman, Daddy. Come get me," his oldest daughter would say.

"I'm coming, baby. I don't know why she's doing me like this," Cedric said, and he had a good laugh about it, but he knew that he had this coming for a long time. He had run this game on Thalia more times than she could count, and now he was finding out what it felt like.

"It's no fun being left alone," she would say on nights when Cedric would be out until midnight.

Midnight seemed to be his line in the sand. No matter what woman he had been with, Cedric made sure that he was home before midnight. Guaranteed. Erica, who seemed to be his preferred cheating partner, knew he wanted to be home by midnight, so she gave him no problem about leaving her apartment.

"Hi, Mom," Sylvie shouted the second Thalia came in from the garage.

"Hey, everybody," she said and looked at Cedric.

He looked as if he was fit to be tied. The look on his face screamed, "I've been waiting for two hours with these kids, and I got someplace to be." Thalia looked at her daughter and winked at her. She rolled her eyes in response.

"Where you been?" Cedric spat out.

"With a client."

"What client?"

Thalia looked at Cedric as if he should have known better than to ask her questions of her. "Michael Wilkerson, you know, the account we're doing the audit for."

"Are we doing an audit?"

"What's that supposed to mean?" Thalia asked as if it was a stupid question to ask.

"Seems to me like you're handling that account by yourself for some reason," Cedric said, and Thalia looked at him as if he had lost his natural mind.

"What's that supposed to mean?" Thalia asked because it was a stupid question.

"It means you seem to be handling this account by yourself."

"Cedric, you know you are more than welcome to come down there with the team and jump in." Thalia laughed loud and hearty. "We could always use the help. Don't sit there and act like you have no say in our business."

When Thalia got up from the kitchen table, she went into the bedroom. Cedric, with an angry look washed over his face, got up from the table and followed her. There was a big difference in their argument management styles. Where it seemed as if she weren't paying attention, Thalia could tell you exactly what you said and were doing.

He walked into the room and slammed the door. "Are you cheating on me?"

Thalia looked at him as if he had lost his mind to even part his lips to say something like that to her. "Of course not," Thalia said with her hand in the air to testify that she had been a good girl. Cedric looked at her because that was how he answered her when she would ask that very same question.

"Are you cheating on me?" Thalia would sometimes ask, and he would get that same look on his face.

"Of course not," he would say in that very same voice, and she'd look at him with those eyes like she was doing at that very moment, knowing full well that he had just left Erica's low-rent apartment and now he came home to break her off some.

Thalia always marveled at the fact that her husband could fuck another woman and then come home and break her back.

"Every time," Thalia said aloud.

He would use that as his rationale to prove he wasn't cheating on her. He even had her believing that he wasn't cheating on her once upon a time. The illusion was shattered when Erica called the house by accident and left a voicemail.

"It's hard to deny you're cheating on me when your fuck bitch leaves a fuckin' message on my phone," she'd said and slapped the shit outta him. More than once. She'd hit him so many times that night that Cedric had to grab her hands and hold them until Thalia stopped moving.

"Not tonight," Cedric had said.

"Let me go, mutha fucka," she'd shouted and kept landing blows to his face and chest. "And get the fuck outta my fuckin' house."

"Okay," he said at times, and he'd leave the house. "If you say so." Cedric would leave Thalia to wonder if he was on his way to Erica's house or had some new woman she didn't already know. He'd leave the house, and of course he'd be back home by midnight.

"You went back and fucked that bitch again, didn't you?"

"No. I was at Haymakers, the sports bar, watching the Rockets play them fuckin' Lakers."

"Who won?"

"Rockets," he said and was glad that he was with Erica and she, knowing that he was married, didn't trip when he jumped in the shower and ran out of there the second they were finished doing what they did. "They're gonna bounce the Lakers from the playoffs."

"And that will be enough for you?

"Damn, sure would be. You know I hate the Lakers and everything they stand for. Fuck Magic, fuck Kareem, fuck Jerry West, and fuck Elgin Baylor," he said as he took off his clothes and got in bed with her.

Thalia pulled back the covers to reveal that she was finished giving him a hard time and now it was time to fuck. And he did. Cedric put it on her.

It was punishment for talking that shit, Cedric thought as he listened to Thalia cover her mouth to keep from screaming and waking up the children.

Aliza thought something was happening to her mother, and she got out of bed and knocked on the door. "Everything all right in there?"

"Yes!" Thalia said in the throes of an orgasm.

"We're fine," her father shouted and stopped moving. "Take your ass back to bed."

"Yes, Daddy."

The following morning, Thalia dressed in a gathered side midi dress and put on her makeup to go to the medical clinic of the doctors. Cedric was still in bed watching her as she dressed.

"Where you going all dressed up looking all fine and sexy?"

"I don't know about you, but I'm going to work. If you recall, I am working off-site this week at the medical practice."

"With the guy you're having an affair with."

"Are we back on this?"

"We never left. Why can't you just admit that you're cheating on me with this Michael guy?"

Thalia's fists hit her hips. "I'm going to explain this to you one last time, okay? After that, I don't want to hear another word about this. Nothing is going on between me and Michael Wilkerson or any other man," Thalia lied.

And you know what? It felt good. She felt completely and perfectly justified in telling Cedric lies. After all, he had been lying to her for years.

"I'm gone," Thalia shouted on her way to the door.

Chapter Eighteen

When the judge entered the room where the arbitration was to be held, the participants rose to their feet. They were there to settle a slip and fall accident.

"Please, be seated," the judge said. "Are both sides ready to proceed?"

"Yes, Your Honor. Velma Whitney for the plaintiff."

Ciara had faced off against Velma Whitney in court before. Although she won the case handily, Ciara thought she was a formidable attorney, and for that reason, she respected her.

"Ciara Reynolds for the defense."

"You may proceed, Ms. Whitney."

"Thank you, Your Honor. The facts in this case are not in dispute, or at least they shouldn't be. Due to the unquestioned negligence of the defendants, my client suffered an injury to his neck and back." She turned to her client. "In your own words, Mr. Austin, please recount for these proceedings the events that occurred on September seventeenth of the current year."

"I went to Bryant's Grocery Store, and I slipped and fell on the floor."

"Did you see anything in the aisle informing you to take any type of caution against the slippery conditions, Mr. Austin?"

"No, there wasn't."

"But there was a slip and fall risk in that aisle?"

"Yes. But I didn't find that out until a woman came down the aisle with a mop, a bucket, and the caution sign."

"All that happened after the fact?"

"Yes. That's what happened."

"Can you tell the attendees of this arbitration what happened next, Mr. Austin?" Whitney said confidently. It was what she saw as her kill shot.

"She apologized for me falling, and then she called 911."

"Mrs. Shaw acknowledged her responsibility for the accident. Thank you, Mr. Austin. At this time, I would like for the video recording of the event in question to be played for this proceeding and be entered into evidence."

"Granted."

The video recording was played, and it showed Mr. Austin walking down the aisle and falling on the floor.

"Do you have any questions for Mr. Austin, Ms. Reynolds?"

"Not at this time, Your Honor. However, I may have some questions for him later."

"So noted. You may proceed."

"Thank you, Your Honor. Indeed, the facts of the case are not in dispute. I just want to be sure that all of the pertinent facts are revealed in this proceeding. Please, state your name?"

"Aliyah Shaw, and this is my husband, Roger."

"And you are the owners and operators of Bryant's Grocery Store?"

"That's right. We were both miserable in our IT jobs and wanted to work together. So, we quit our jobs, sold our house, and we bought the store."

"How long have you been open?"

"Six months."

"How's it going so far?"

"It was slow at first. People had to get to know we were open. But it's just starting to pick up."

"This is an interesting story, but I fail to see the relevance, Your Honor," Whitney said.

"Unless you're in a hurry to end this proceeding, I'm inclined to allow Ms. Reynolds some leeway here."

"Thank you, Your Honor." Ciara turned to Mrs. Shaw. "Can you tell me, from your point of view, what happened on the date in question before these proceedings, please?"

"I was restocking shelves when I was informed by one of my customers that there was a broken bottle of pickles on aisle three. I went and got a broom and a dustpan, and I cleaned up the breakage."

"What did you do after you swept up the broken glass?"

"I went to get the mop, the bucket, and the caution sign, but when I got back, Mr. Austin had already fallen. I told him to stay down, and I called 911."

"Thank you, Mrs. Shaw. At this time, Your Honor, I would like, with the court's indulgence, to ask Mr. Austin some questions."

"You may proceed."

"Thank you, Your Honor."

Ciara opened the file in front of her and flipped a few pages. Then she looked at Austin. "You're a suer, aren't you, Mr. Austin?"

"What do you mean?"

"You sue people and companies. It's kind of your thing. Isn't that correct, Mr. Austin?"

"Objection, Your Honor. What do Mr. Austin's past encounters with the legal system have to do with the straightforward matter being considered before these proceedings?"

"As I said, Ms. Whitney, I will allow Ms. Reynolds some leeway. However, I trust we're going somewhere with this line of questioning."

"Yes, Your Honor." Ciara smiled confidently because she was about to unveil her kill shot. "I promise to bring the cattle to the barn ridden hard and put away wet, Your Honor."

"Objection overruled. You may proceed, Ms. Reynolds."

"Thank you, Your Honor." Once again, Ciara turned her attention to Mr. Austin. "Let's see." She held up a piece of paper. "You sued a bus company when you fell on their steps." Ciara held up another piece of paper. "And then there was the time when you fell on the ice outside your neighbor's house." She picked up and held a third piece of paper. "Then there was the time while you were working as a school groundskeeper, your golf cart hit a pothole, and the cart tipped over, and you were injured in the fall." Ciara put down the papers. "You're just an unlucky guy bad stuff happens to that you can sue for."

"I think you should know that my patience is running thin, Ms. Reynolds."

"I understand, Your Honor. At this time, I would like for this recording to be played for the court and entered into evidence."

"Is this the same video recording that was already entered into evidence?" the judge asked.

"A longer, more complete version, Your Honor."

"Proceed."

"Thank you, Your Honor."

Ciara began the recording. "Please note the time stamp as five minutes prior to the starting point of the one previously entered into evidence. Here, you can clearly see Mr. Austin on the aisle in question. And, as you can clearly see, that is also Mr. Austin picking up and dropping the pickle jar on the floor before leaving the aisle and returning once Mrs. Shaw gets up the broken glass."

"I think I've seen enough," the judge said. "Mr. Austin, your case is dismissed. And you are so ordered to pay court costs and attorney fees. We're done here."

"Thank you, Your Honor," Ciara said as the judge exited the conference room.

"Good find," Whitney said to Ciara when they shook hands.

"We found it purely by accident. We had cued it up the day before, and we were talking when we saw it."

"Anyway, congratulations. You want to grab a drink later?"

"Not today. I already have plans. Rain check?"

"Sure," Whitney said and walked out with her client, wondering why he couldn't be honest with her, and they left the conference room.

"Thank you, Ms. Reynolds," Mrs. Shaw said to her, and she hugged her. "Our insurance rates would have gone through the roof if he had gotten away with this."

After spending the afternoon in arbitration, it was time to relax. Ciara met Savannah at Gourmet Gaze for dinner and drinks. It wasn't going to be all relaxing, at least not for Savannah. The following afternoon, Savannah was meeting with officials from the Securities and Exchange Commission. Ciara would be by her side, along with Thalia. Therefore, this was meant to be a strategy session. That was until Thalia said she couldn't make it.

"But I'll be right there by your side tomorrow," Thalia promised.

Therefore, it was just Ciara and Savannah having girl talk over grilled T-bone steaks and lobster tails.

"And I'll have a Mai Tai," Ciara ordered.

"Make it two," Savannah added.

"What do you think is up with Thalia missing our little strategy session?" Ciara asked.

"Probably had a hot date with Griffin," Savannah suggested.

"You're probably right." Ciara sipped her water. "I'm happy for her."

"As long as she's happy, I couldn't be happier for her."

And Thalia was making herself happy, for maybe the first time since she said, "I do," and became Mrs. Thalia Blackburn. But if her girls only knew that it wasn't Griffin who was making her happy. She hadn't seen him in weeks. Even though the audit of his practice was completed, Thalia met Michael for dinner almost every night.

"What about you? Are you happy, Savannah?"

"I'll be happy when all this is behind me."

"I meant in your personal life. What's going on with you and Milo? And, yes, this is me officially being nosy. So, give it up."

"We're doing fine. We talk every day, at least once, and he's been here just about every weekend."

"And the sex?"

"Awesome, every time. What about you? How are you doing since the breakup?"

"Honestly, Zack broke my heart."

Savannah reached out and touched her hand. "I'm sorry, Ciara."

"But I'm moving forward with my life. But it hurts. Some days more than others. How could I have not known the man I was with for two years was gay?"

It was the singular question that Ciara continued to ask herself but didn't have an answer for. Therefore, as she told Savannah, she was moving forward with her life. Which, at this point, was that at the end of the evening, Ciara would go home alone, take a hot shower, and get into bed. She'd select a porno video with two women and a man, get Ava from the drawer, and masturbate until she screamed and drifted off to sleep. That was the plan for that evening.

However, while she was in the shower, Ciara thought back to the woman she used to be before she met Zack. She used to date. "Now all you do is masturbate," she said aloud.

Since she'd broken up with Zack, Ciara had sex a few times with Rahim Dalton. But the more she got to know him, the less Ciara liked him. "But he does have that big, pretty dick working in his favor. And his head game ain't bad either."

Therefore, he became an occasional convenience to be used as needed. When Ciara got out of the shower, instead of preparing for another night with Ava, she went into her dressing room. When she emerged, Ciara was wearing a pair of Marguerite high-rise skinny jeans and a jacket by L'Agence that she was rocking with a pair of Christian Louboutin red bottom leather pumps.

Thirty minutes later, Ciara was sitting at the bar at a spot called Mentara. She was sipping a Mai Tai when a handsome man with short hair and a goatee stood next to her.

"Is this seat taken?"

"It will be when you sit down."

He smiled at Ciara. "I guess it's taken then," he said and sat down next to her.

"What are you drinking?" the bartender asked.

"Absolut and water."

"You ready for another Mai Tai?"

"Go ahead and bring me another."

"Put it on my tab."

"Thank you, that is very nice of you, Mr. . . ."

"Thompson. Jack Thompson."

"Ciara Reynolds," she said, and the conversation took off from there. It led to an exchange of cell numbers and a promise to get together and do something. However, when Jack excused himself to go to the men's room, another man approached.

"You wanna dance?"

"I would love to dance."

Therefore, when Jack returned from the men's room, he saw Ciara on the dance floor. He reclaimed his seat at the bar and hoped she was coming back because Ciara was fine and he had spent his money on her.

Shit, just for a hug and a kiss on the cheek, he thought.

When the song was over, he watched and waited for a while as Ciara talked up the man with whom she had danced. On her way out of the club, Ciara passed Jack at the bar.

"Call me," she said as she walked out with the other man. He walked her to her car. Once they exchanged numbers, Ciara went home, thinking about her return to the dating scene. There was a time before Zack when Ciara kept a stable of three or four men: one she could talk to, two she went out on dates with depending on what she was in the mood to do, and one fuck buddy. His name was Charles. They never went anywhere, and they never did anything other than fuck.

"I wonder . . ." she said and dialed his number.

"Ciara?"

"Yes."

"What's up?"

"You alone?"

"Yeah, why?"

"Can I come get in bed with you?"

"Shit, yeah. I'll text you my new address."

The following evening, Ciara met Jared Clarke at an Italian bistro called Prime di Carrara. Coincidently, it was one of Zack's favorite places to take her.

"Take your head out of his ass," Ciara said, remembering that she was moving on from Zack. Ciara would no longer be his fool.

Never again.

Over manicotti baked to perfection and cannelloni, Ciara and FBI Special Agent Clarke talked a little about this and that. She found him to be knowledgeable on a number of topics, from politics and current events to the environment to the state of black people in America. The two talked about some of their hobbies. Ciara told him about her recent travel experience to Saint Barts. Naturally, she left out the more interesting moments of her trip. He talked in detail about his new interest in skydiving.

"That sounds exciting."

"It is. You should let me take you up sometime. It's an experience you'll never forget."

"I'll bet."

They talked about their upbringing in small south Texas towns and the values they shared being from those places. Ciara found him to be the most interesting man she'd met in years.

"I enjoyed you tonight," Ciara leaned across the table to say.

"I enjoyed being with you too. In fact, I'd love to see a lot more of you."

"As much as I'd like to say I want that too, right now that is not where my head is."

"Where is your head?"

"That's the thing. I don't know, and that is largely because I don't know who Ciara Reynolds is anymore. I know the woman I used to be. But the pretty woman I've been avoiding making eye contact with in the mirror, her I don't know. You see, I was engaged for years."

"I remember. He gave you the ring the day before I came to see you."

"Sitting in there trying to conduct business, and there I am out in the hallway, showing off my ring."

"It was a nice ring if memory serves."

"It serves you well. But I hope you understand that I need to find the woman I was and reclaim her before I can move forward. Ciara Reynolds is in here somewhere. I just need to find out who that is now."

"I understand."

"Do you?"

"I do," Jared said.

"You don't know that you do or even could."

"Why is that?"

"I really can't see you submerging your entire personality to be with a woman."

"Honestly, I could not even imagine doing that."

"And what woman would want you to? I know I wouldn't want a man I could control and manipulate into doing what I wanted him to do. But I'll be honest with you, there were times that I felt more like property than I was in a relationship," she said sadly and sipped her drink. "We went where he wanted to go. We did what he wanted to do when he wanted to do it. And only if he wanted to do it. If it was something that I wanted to do, it was, 'We'll see.' So, you see, I need to rediscover who Ciara Reynolds is, and then I'll have that Ciara Reynolds to give to someone. But now, I am on a mission of rediscovery. Does that make sense?"

"It does. Actually, it makes a lot of sense. No man, no real man anyway, wants to be with a woman who doesn't know who she is. I'm looking for a confident black woman who knows who she is and what her worth is." He chuckled, and Ciara enjoyed the robust sound of his laughter. "I wouldn't want a woman I could control and manipulate into doing what I wanted."

"I think you made that point plain when you said you were looking for a confident black woman. I took that to mean a strong woman. In every way possible."

"You might find this hard to believe, but I was born into a matriarchal family on both sides of my family. The women run things, make all the decisions, and they control the money. The men, well, they have other concerns to deal with just being men."

"Like what?"

"Playing poker, chasing women, drinking liquor, hunting, fishing, and riding that big-ass John Deere tractor."

Ciara laughed. "Your folks never let you get near that tractor, did they?"

"Oh, hell no. Not even close."

Ciara giggled as if she were a schoolgirl with a crush on an older man. However, if she had to guess, she would say that he was in his early to mid-forties. Ciara found the evening with Jared Clarke stimulating. She considered herself to be an intelligent woman, not just someplace to bust nuts in. All Zack wanted to talk about, other than his cases, which he would, ad nauseam at times, the only thing he wanted to talk about were the local sports teams. The Rockets, Astros, even the Texans and them damn Cowboys and choke artist Dak Prescott, the Dallas Cowboys quarterback.

But Ciara found it both fascinating and stimulating when Jared began telling her about the missions he was a part of when he was a field agent in Mexico. Those stories of courage and patriotism appealed to her, and it made Ciara want him. But this new "trying to find her way back to herself" Ciara was just dating. Although she was sure that he would rise in position, that made Mr. Jared Clarke number four on the depth chart behind Rahim and the two men she had met at the club before. And Charles, of course, may eliminate the need for Rahim.

"Good night, Jared."

"Good night, Ciara." He opened her door. "I want you to know that I heard every word you said, and I respect it."

"Good for you."

"So, if it's all right with you, beautiful Ciara, I'd like to be around to help you pick up the pieces until we put Ciara together. I am interested in seeing what that's gonna look like when it's done."

"I'd like to see that too. So, we'll see how that works out for you," she said with a polite girlfriend hug and a kiss on the cheek.

Chapter Nineteen

Upon arrival early at the doctor's office, before the rest of the staff got there, Thalia was greeted by Michael in the lobby. He had arranged for them to have breakfast in his office.

"I didn't know if you ate already, but . . ." He opened the door to his office. "I took the liberty of having something sent in."

When Thalia stepped into the office, she saw the spread that Michael arranged for her. The breakfast spread, which he had to have hired a caterer for, included quiche, paninis with ham, French toast casserole, a smoked salmon platter, scones, fresh fruit salad, yogurt, coffee, and black and herbal teas.

"Wow. All this."

Thalia looked into Michael's eyes. Although she thought that Dr. Michael Wilkerson was one fine-ass man, she never thought he'd be interested in her: a married, 36-year-old mother of three.

I guess I was wrong.

She did tell him about her cheating husband and the fact that she had considered getting a divorce.

"I hope I'm not being too forward."

"Not at all," she said because there was a chance that she was misinterpreting his intentions. *This all could be perfectly innocent. He may just like to eat and this is something he does.*

"I didn't eat breakfast, and I'm hungry," Thalia said, and once she fixed her plate, she sat down in one of the chairs in front of Michael's desk.

"The staff can have whatever we don't eat," Michael said as he got a plate for himself and sat down. Everything was wonderful. When they finished eating, the rest of the staff began arriving. Michael greeted them as they came in and told them there was food in his office.

When Thalia came out of the office, she walked up to Michael. "Since your office is in use, I'll work in the conference room today. That won't be a problem, will it?"

"Not at all."

Thalia got the things she'd need for the day and headed for the conference room.

As the day wore on, Thalia conducted her interviews with the staff concerning their individual positions, looking for the source of the problem. Based on what Cedric said and her own experience, the interview she was looking forward to was with Emily Sloan, the woman they hired to manage the office and deal with Medicare. But she wanted to speak with the rest of the staff before she got around to Emily.

It was just after three when Michael drifted into the conference room. "Good afternoon, Doctor."

"How's it going?"

"Well."

"Still don't want to tell me what you think?"

Thalia stood up. "I need to stretch my legs. As I said, it wouldn't be a comprehensive review," she said, knowing that she wanted to interview Emily Sloan before she drew any conclusions.

"Do you have any plans for dinner this evening?"

"I do not."

"Would you like to have dinner with me this evening?"

"I would love to have dinner with you," Thalia said and thought that she needed to change some part of her program. Michael had just invited her to have dinner with him. To Thalia, that meant that he was interested in her and not just as an auditor. Dr. Michael Wilkerson was interested in Thalia, the woman.

"Great. I'll be ready after my last patient leaves," he said and left the conference room.

When he left, Thalia got her purse, and she left the office. When she got to the house, she had enough time to change before the children got home from school. The last person to come into the house was her 12-year-old daughter, Aliza.

When she saw what her mother was wearing, she asked, "Where are you going dressed like that?" Aliza asked about the Zimmermann Balance cargo belted midi dress Thalia was wearing.

"I'm having dinner this evening with a client."

Aliza frowned. "Are you taking us to Mrs. Johnson again?"

"No. I think you are old enough to stay here by yourself and be responsible for your brother and sister. But what do you think?"

Hearing that was music to her ears. Aliza had long since believed that she was responsible enough to be home alone and take care of her younger siblings. "I think I'm responsible enough, Mommy."

"Okay. Don't disappoint me."

"I won't, Mommy, I promise."

Thalia hugged Aliza. "I know you won't. You're too much like me to disappoint me."

Aliza laughed and hugged her mother a little tighter. "I am still your mini me."

"Tell your father I'll be home at ten," she said on her way to the door.

"I will," Aliza said, walking alongside her mother.

"You look nice, Mommy," Eric said.

"Thank you."

Thalia got in her car and drove back to the doctor's office. When she got there, Michael had just finished up with his last patient and was ready to go to dinner.

"You look amazing, Thalia," Michael said the second he saw her.

"Thank you, Michael. So, where are you taking me?"

"We're having dinner at Rainbow Lodge."

"I've always wanted to go there. Wild game, steak, and seafood."

"I think you'll like it. It's a log cabin along the banks of the White Oak Bayou."

"'Right in the heart of Houston,'" Thalia said, quoting the advertisement for the restaurant, and she followed Michael out of the office to his car.

Of course he's driving the Jaguar.

Michael opened Thalia's door, and she got in his white 1969 Jaguar XKE coupe.

The meal was amazing, and the two laughed and talked throughout and found that they were a lot alike in so many ways.

"There's something I want to say, but I'm not sure if this is the right time or even if there is a good time to say this to you," Michael began nervously.

Thalia sat up a little straighter. "This sounds serious, Michael," she said and sipped her wine.

"It is." Michael paused and looked at Thalia. "I don't know if you felt it, but from the second I saw you, I've felt that there was, for lack of a better word, an energy between us."

"I've felt it too."

Although her answer was exactly what he wanted to hear, Michael was surprised that she admitted it. "You have?"

"Yes, Michael. I've felt the energy between us each time you've looked at me or spoken to me."

Michael reached across the table and took Thalia's hands in his. "I know you told me that you're married, and you have three children, and your husband cheats on you, and you were thinking about filing for divorce. I just want you to know that if and when you do separate yourself from the situation, I would be very interested in seeing if you and I could have something together."

Thalia was blown away. That was the last thing she expected to hear.

"Yes, Michael. I am all those things. I'm a married mother of three with a cheating husband. All that is true." She squeezed his hand. "But I am also a woman. A woman who wants and needs to be loved by a man who loves her."

"I believe, wholeheartedly, that I could be that man for you." Michael squeezed Thalia's hands in his and looked into her eyes. "If I were your man, I would spend every minute of every day giving you so much to love. And I would spend all that time loving you."

Thalia giggled as if she were a schoolgirl with a crush. "And I would let you do it and bask in every magnificent second of it," Thalia said and allowed herself to get caught up in the fantasy picture of life that Michael had just painted.

"I would never cheat on you. My God, why would I? You are the most beautiful and sexy woman I've ever seen."

"Now you're pushing it." Thalia laughed. "I know there are plenty of women out there more beautiful and sexier than me."

"Beauty is in the eye of the beholder."

"True."

"And what I behold is your beauty."

"You know what?"

"What?"

"I'm going to stop arguing with you. I am a beautiful and sexy woman who the very handsome and sexy man sitting across from me is interested in."

"More than just interested. I'm serious about this."

"Well, I guess we'll see just how serious you are."

As their evening together drew to a close, Michael paid the check, and they left the restaurant and walked hand in hand to his car. After he had announced his intentions and said everything to Thalia except "I love you," she thought they were going to his place or a hotel so he could make sweet love to her. But that was not what happened. What happened surprised her, but it definitely let her know that Michael was serious about what he was saying to her.

When they got back to the medical office, Michael parked next to her car and got out. There was still a chance that he just wanted her to get her car so she could follow him to their destination, where he would make sweet love to her. But that wasn't to be either. Michael opened her door and held out his hand to help her out of the car. Still holding hands, they made the short walk to her car.

"There is nothing I want more than to take you home with me and make love to you."

And I want you to.

"But I know that I have to respect the fact that you are a married woman. So, I'll say good night."

"Good night, Michael," Thalia said sadly instead of insisting that he didn't need to respect the fact that she was married at all and he should take her home so they could make love.

As badly as I want to and want him.

So, a now sexually frustrated Thalia got in her car and drove home. It was about that time that Cedric arrived at home and was greeted by Aliza. She was sitting in the living room alone, watching TV. Now that she was in charge, she made her younger sister and brother go to bed so she could watch the TV herself.

"Hey, baby girl," Cedric said.

"Hey, Daddy."

"Where's your mother? I didn't see her car when I came in."

"She went out."

"And she didn't take y'all to Mrs. Johnson?"

"No. She said that I was old enough to be here by myself and be responsible for Eric and Sylvie," Aliza said proudly, thinking that her father would be happy that she was taking on more responsibility.

"No, you're not." Cedric shook his head. "You're just a baby your damn self. What could she be thinking?"

Aliza bounced up angrily from the couch. "Mommy thinks I'm old enough," she said and stormed out of the room.

"Well, she's wrong!" Cedric shouted.

"Yes, I am old enough not to need a babysitter!" Aliza yelled and slammed her bedroom door.

It was thirty minutes later when Thalia came through the door. When she went into the living room, Cedric was sitting there mean mugging. Thalia wanted to cover her mouth and laugh as she wondered if that was what she looked like all those nights when it was she sitting in that very spot waiting for Cedric to come through the door so she could ask that all-important question.

"Where you been?" Cedric asked.

"I had dinner this evening with Dr. Wilkerson."

"Dressed like that, I know it was no business dinner."

"No, it wasn't. I mean, it started out that way, but then we agreed to talk about what was going on in his office in the morning." She sat down on the couch next to

Cedric, kicked off her heels, put her head on his shoulder, and proceeded to lie to him. "It was supposed to be a celebration because I've wrapped up the audit."

"And?"

"You were right. The office manager, Emily Sloan. She had partitioned the hard drive on her computer. Once I brought somebody in to access it, I found four transactions, each for over twenty-five thousand dollars for services billed but never performed." That part was true. "But Dr. Wilkerson decided that he wanted to enjoy the evening's meal and talk shop in the office in the morning."

"What y'all talk about after that?"

"You know me, I babbled on endlessly about the kids," she lied, and since Cedric didn't challenge her on it, Thalia assumed that he bought it hook, line, and sinker.

Chapter Twenty

Savannah was excited. It was Friday night, and lately, that only meant one thing to her. *Milo will be here tonight.*

"Evening, Oscar."

"Good evening, Ms. Ayers," her chauffeur replied as he held the door open for her to get in.

"Thank you."

Once Savannah was in, Oscar shut the door and came around the limousine to get in. It was Friday; therefore, he knew where they were going.

"Where to this evening, Ms. Ayers?"

"Airport."

"On our way," he said and put the vehicle in gear.

On the drive to the airport, Savannah looked out the window and thought about her week as president at Intuitive Energy. As was the case for presidents of most companies, her primary responsibility would be the company's financial management, the formulation and execution of the company's financial plan. However, Savannah was, and she believed intentionally, kept out of that area of operations, and she was not invited to financial meetings. Even though she had a very good idea of what was going on in those meetings, Savannah chose to keep her head down and do the job they hired her for.

"We need to adapt so we can meet the demands and complexities of the remote and hybrid workplace," Savannah said at a meeting with Lauren Beard, the vice president of human resources, and Fynn McKenzie, vice president of IT.

"Right now, my largest concern is keeping remote and hybrid teams connected and engaged," Lauren said.

"How do you propose we overcome problems with that?" Savannah asked.

"I don't know," she giggled.

Lauren Beard was one of the smartest people and most effective VPs at Intuitive Energy, but the way she giggled between sometimes brilliant sentences got on Savannah's nerves.

"With the collaboration of engaging team building activities. I think that will assist in helping managers ensure that remote employees remain productive and accountable."

"That sounds good. Do you have a plan to implement that strategy?" Savannah asked. "Because I believe that effective communication is going to be key here."

"I agree. The most effective way to overcome any barrier is to maintain clear and consistent communication," she giggled, and it got on Savannah's nerves. "But to answer your question, the plan is in development. As soon as it's finished, I will email it to you, and we can meet to discuss it."

"Time frame?"

"Give me a week."

"A week it is." Savannah then turned to Fynn McKenzie. "Are you prepared to implement her plan once it's completed?"

"I believe we are. Of course, I would need to see it. But I feel confident that the expanded use of the tools at our disposal will be up to the task."

"And those tools are?"

"By using platforms like Slack, Microsoft Teams, or Zoom to facilitate our communication between management and the employees," Fynn said, "it has the potential to improve issue response time because they would have the ability to send a message via Slack and get a response almost immediately. Of course, that depends largely on who the manager is, but in theory, that's how it should work."

"Have you met some of our managers?" Lauren said and giggled.

"I have. Why do you think I included the words 'that depends largely on who the manager is'?" Everybody laughed. "That, and the use of shared knowledge bases facilitating information sharing should cut down on the need to ask a lot of questions because that information should be available in the knowledge base."

"Some departments will have to dramatically expand their knowledge base to be able to accommodate that," Lauren said.

"Make it so," Savannah ordered. "We need to establish clear policies and guidelines for remote and hybrid working. Therefore, in addition to everything else on your plate, I am tasking you with developing a comprehensive remote work policy that outlines expectations, work hours, and communication protocols."

"Thanks."

Fynn chuckled. "You know no act of efficiency and effectiveness goes unpunished."

"Tell me about it," Lauren said.

"Anything else for me?" Savannah asked.

"If I had anything, I wouldn't bring it up now," Fynn said. "I've got too much on my big-ass plate already."

"And I don't?" Lauren said quickly, and Savannah stood up.

"That's all, folks," she said and left the conference room.

It was also Savannah's responsibility to meet with the managers of the company. She hated those meetings because they almost always devolved into complaint sessions. That's why Savannah began bringing her admin, Kiera, to those meetings. Her job was to note all the complaints so Savannah could address them with that department's VP.

"As a product manager, my problems are caused by workflow mismanagement," Pamela Hardy stated. "That is going to involve communication between every member of the organization at the same time."

"Lauren and Fynn are working on developing a solution to that. Communication is a company-wide issue that I plan on putting to bed," Savannah said and hoped that addressed Pamela's issue. If it didn't, they might be there for hours listening to her drone on about her problems.

"The energy between teams affects the development speed and quality of the final product," Pamela said.

"As we are well aware, Pamela," Savannah said sternly and once again hoped that would shut her down.

"I think that means shut up, Pam, so we can move on," Kyle Miles, who managed the sales department, said.

When Savannah laughed, everybody else in the meeting did as well. "I wouldn't have put it quite that way, but we do need to move on."

That was a part of the week Savannah had. As a consequence, she was more than ready for the weekend. Even more excited to see Milo.

When they arrived at the airport, Oscar got out and waited for Milo to come outside of the terminal. The second he saw him, Oscar held up the sign that said HENDERSON.

Once he saw the sign, Milo walked to the limousine.

"Evening, Oscar," Milo said and handed Oscar his luggage.

"Good evening, Mr. Henderson. How was your flight?"

"Smooth. It gave me a chance to catch some z's," Milo said, and Oscar opened the door. "Thank you," Milo said and got in.

"Hi," Savannah cooed softly.

Milo leaned in and kissed her. "Hi yourself."

Oscar got in and lowered the glass partition between the front and back of the limousine. "Where to, Ms. Ayers?"

"Take me home, please, Oscar."

"On our way," he replied, raised the partition, and drove on.

"How was your flight?" Savannah asked.

"I was just telling Oscar that it was a smooth flight, so it gave me a chance to catch some z's."

"Good. I need you rested." She had given some thought to having sex with Milo in the limousine on the way to the house. Savannah quickly dismissed that thought. *Things like that have a funny way of getting out and becoming breakroom gossip, so it ain't happening.* She looked at Milo, and Savannah exhaled at the thought of it.

"What?"

"You'll see."

When Oscar brought Milo's luggage into the house, Savannah told him that was it for the evening and that she would call him with tomorrow's agenda in the morning. He said good night, and she locked the door behind him.

"Alone at last," Milo said.

However, he was not prepared when Savannah rushed toward him and into his arms.

"That means you're in trouble, buddy." She kissed him. It was not much more than a peck.

"Am I now?"

"You are. But I know that you are just the man to call when the trouble requires a big solution."

"Is that a fact?"

"It is." Savannah kissed him again. This time, it was long and passionate. "You know, I love that you're strong enough to carry me."

"Well, your ex was a good guy, but he wasn't exactly what I'd call muscular."

"Go on and say it. The boy was skinny and weak."

"You married him."

"And he divorced me."

"To my grateful benefit."

"So, you know what I think you should do? I mean, like, right now?"

"What's that?"

"Take me upstairs, strip me down, and take care of this big problem."

Without saying another word, Milo did as he was asked. He not only carried her upstairs and stripped her down, but Milo also took her into the bathroom. He turned on the shower as Savannah smiled. Once it was a good temperature, Milo turned to Savannah.

"Undress me."

Savannah took her time and undressed Milo slowly. They stepped into the shower, and she started to step into his strong arms, but Milo turned to get the loofah and the soap. He then took his time bathing every inch of Savannah.

"See what happens when I get some sleep and not work on the plane?" he said as he dried her.

"You need to shut up and fuck me."

"That was my plan," Milo said, and Savannah put her finger over his lips.

"No more talk."

She looked at Milo. His eyes were on fire. That let her know how much he wanted her. Savannah's body hummed with electricity. Milo pulled her to him, and she pressed into him. He was hard for her.

Only me.

Savannah rubbed her body against his erection, making him harder as they kissed fervently. Their mouths seemed as if they were fused together as their tongues danced. Milo squeezed her ass, and her hands explored his body. Savannah clasped her hands together before placing them around his throbbing dick. She pumped his erection up and down, steadily increasing her pace as Milo swelled in her hands.

Milo enjoyed watching Savannah pleasuring him, so he propped up his pillow and watched Savannah use her tongue to explore his shaft. She licked him up and down before taking him into her mouth. She ran her tongue around the head.

"Yes," he groaned.

That groan ran through Savannah, causing her to shudder. Her own seduction was doing her in. This was supposed to be about her pleasing him.

I only know one way to do this, she thought and took Milo once again to the back of her throat.

"Damn," Milo said and grabbed a handful of sheets.

But make no mistake about it, Savannah wanted him inside of her so badly that her hands were shaking.

Milo pulled her up and laid her out on the bed. He moved over her and started to caress Savannah's body. He started sucking her toes, making her squirm on top of the sheets. He blazed a trail to her thighs, stopping before he met her wetness.

He spread her lips apart before running circles around Savannah's clit. She wanted to scream because he was so close to making her explode. He penetrated her with his fingers, moving in and out of her before finally moving in with his tongue. Milo flicked her clit over and over and gently sucked on it until she exploded.

Once Savannah caught her breath, she looked at the confident smile on Milo's face.

Made you cum, what you gonna do?

"You're in big trouble now."

"Bring it."

And she did. Savannah brought it long and strong, and Milo had to admit that he was glad to have slept on the flight from New York.

"So, what do you want to do this weekend?" Savannah asked because their relationship had gotten to the point where they wanted to do things together other than just fuck all weekend.

"I wanna go to the beach."

"We can ride down to Surfside Beach. It's about seventy miles away," she began, and Milo kissed her mouth shut.

"No, Savannah. I wanna go to a beach. Not a strip of sand and some dirty water. I'm talking about a nice Caribbean beach with crystal-clear water."

"That would be nice," Savannah said and rolled into his arms.

"Pick an island."

"Let me see."

"One you haven't been to."

"That makes it a little harder."

"Oh. You want me to make it harder for you to decide." Milo kissed her.

"No. that is not what I meant, but go ahead, have your way with me."

"Stop stalling and tell me what island you want to go to, Savannah."

"Okay. I've never been to Barbados," she said and reached for Milo just as he got out of bed.

"Where are my pants?"

"Where are you going?"

"Nowhere. I just need my phone."

"They're in the bathroom. Remember, 'Undress me'?"

Milo pointed. "Right." He went into the bathroom.

"What do you need your phone for?"

Milo came back to bed with his phone. "Because I don't have my laptop, and I promised Jodie that I would not call her for any reason."

"What are you looking up?"

"Resorts in Barbados."

"Huh?"

"You said you wanted to go to Barbados, right?"

"Right."

"Well, we gotta stay somewhere, right?"

"Right."

"So, unless you're gonna call Kiera, this is how we find a place to stay."

"Right."

For the next thirty minutes or so, Savannah and Milo browsed resorts. They settled on the O2 Beach Club & Spa. However, when Milo was about to click to make a reservation, Savannah stopped him.

"What?" he asked.

"We haven't even picked a date."

Milo looked at her. "I was talking about today."

"Today?"

"Yes, Savannah, today."

"You're talking about us flying to Barbados today?"

"Yes."

"And coming back tomorrow?"

"No." Milo looked Savannah directly in her beautiful eyes. "I can take a week off. What about you, Madam President?"

Savannah thought about it. "Maybe not a week. How about we leave today and you have me back for work on Wednesday?"

"I'll take it," Milo said and booked a room at the O2 Beach Club & Spa.

Chapter Twenty-one

Since the day that Michael walked into Thalia's life, it had been as if she were walking on a fluffy cloud. What was both good and bad about it was that everybody noticed the change in her attitude.

The first ones to notice were Aliza, Eric, and Sylvie. It began one afternoon when she came home from the office. Thalia came into the house and found them sitting in the living room. The television wasn't on. They were just sitting there.

"Hey, y'all." Nobody said a word. "What's wrong?" When Aliza and Sylvie looked at Eric, Thalia said, "Follow me."

Knowing what was coming next, Aliza and Sylvie started giggling, that was until their mother looked back at them with the evil eye. The giggling stopped, and there were no more smiles to be seen on their faces.

"I didn't think so," their mother said and then continued to lead their brother to the bedroom to await his fate.

"What's going on with you?"

"I got into a fight at school, and I got suspended," he said, expecting the legendary Thalia madness to begin. But it didn't. When it didn't come, Eric continued, "You see, there's this girl."

Thalia held up her hand. "Please tell me this ain't about some nappy-head little girl."

"It is. Her name is LaShawn, but yeah, Ma, it's about a girl."

Thalia shook her head. "Go on."

"Me and her were in the cafeteria having lunch when this guy Eddie came in with his crew."

"Who's Eddie?"

"He used to be her boyfriend, but they broke up."

"Go on."

"One of his boys sees us and taps Eddie. When he looks, he sees us. LaShawn says, 'Here they come. Let me handle it.'"

"How old is this little nappy-head girl anyway?"

"Her name is LaShawn, and she's twelve."

"Go on."

"Him and his crew rush to the table, and he gets in my face. He says, 'What you doing with my girl?' LaShawn bounces up, and she gets in his face and says, 'I ain't your girl.' When everyone around hears that, they start laughing. He grabs me by my shirt and pulls me out of my chair." Eric paused. "I remembered what you said about trying to de-escalate the situation, and I said, 'Get your hands off me.'"

Eric had actually said, "Get your mutha fuckin' hands off me, nigga," but we'll pass that for now.

"And he swung on me. I blocked the punch, and . . ." Eric began smiling, and Thalia wondered why. "I hit him so hard that it busted his nose, and it started bleeding."

"Go on," Thalia said, and now she knew what he was smiling about.

"Then the teachers came running over, and I got suspended because they didn't see he started it."

"They never do." Thalia shook her head. "Go on."

"He got to go back to class, laughing at me."

Instead of yelling as she usually did, Thalia nodded and stood up. "I'm gonna go up to the school and straighten this out. And I'm going to talk to your teachers because you are not gonna fall behind because of this foolishness."

She shook her head. "Over some nappy-head little girl."

"Her name is LaShawn, but thank you, Ma," Eric said, shocked that his mother hadn't lost her mind, as was her custom.

"You're welcome," she said and opened the door to find her daughters sitting on the floor at the door. "What y'all doing?"

"Nothing, Mommy."

"All right," Thalia said and continued down the hall.

Aliza and Sylvie watched their mother walk down the hall. They looked in the room at Eric. He shrugged his shoulders because they were all expecting her legendary Thalia madness and tongue-lashings all around that usually came with it. But there was nothing. Not a word.

The next one to notice her new attitude was Cedric. It happened when Thalia came into the office one morning. There were two dozen roses on her desk. Thalia went into the office, picked up the card, and read it.

Thalia,

I understand that your husband is probably going to see these and get jealous. I hope he asks you about it, and I hope you tell him this is from a man who appreciates you for you and treats you the way you deserve to be treated.

Enjoy your day.

Thalia smiled when she read the card, had a good laugh to herself, ripped the card into pieces, put the pieces into her purse to dispose of once she was out of the office, and sat down at her desk. However, when Cedric got to the office, Esther Edwards, who Thalia had always believed was his office snitch, walked straight to Cedric and pointed to Thalia's office. She had to laugh when she saw his eyes narrow, and he headed straight for her office.

"Hey, Cedric."

"Hey. Who sent you them flowers?"

"Michael and Aurora Wilkerson thanked me for a job well done because I was able to, with your help"—she nodded in recognition—"identify the source of their problem." And then she flipped it on him. "So, these flowers are as much for you as they are for me, Cedric."

"Then you aren't fuckin' this nigga?"

"No, Cedric. I am not fucking Michael," she was able to say honestly because he had asked her the wrong question. What he should have asked was whether she was fuckin' anybody, and based on the mood she was in, Thalia might have just told him the truth. It wasn't Michael she had been fuckin'. It was a married man named Griffin. Since that night in the car, Thalia hadn't heard from Aston.

"Are you still cheating on me with Erica?" she asked in a tone of voice that wasn't the angry, accusatory voice.

"No, Thalia. I am not cheating on you."

Thalia chuckled. "Then we have no problem, do we?"

"No." Cedric dropped his head and walked out of her office, feeling defeated.

"Talk to you later, Cedric."

"Right," he said, feeling confused about what just happened. He had expected Thalia to lose her mind when she brought up Erica. But she didn't.

Later that night, Thalia took her children to the Harris County Fair and Rodeo. As they wandered around the fairgrounds, she saw that Michael was there with his niece and nephews. They were in line to get cotton candy.

When she saw him, they introduced each other to the children. And then they spoke. Thalia told him that her daughter Aliza was a snitch.

"Daddy's girl, huh?"

"She will call and tell him everything."

Thalia looked to see that Aliza was staring at Michael's nephew Jerome, but she was on her phone.

"Probably talking to him now."

"Well, I tell you what, after we get our cotton candy, I'll say it was nice meeting you and leave you to enjoy the fair with your kids."

"Would you?"

"No problem."

After Michael left, Aliza told Thalia, "Daddy wants to talk to you."

"Snitch." Thalia took the phone. "Hello, Cedric."

"You out with that nigga?"

"No, Cedric. I am here at the fair with our children. Michael is here with his niece and his nephews."

"But y'all planned to meet there, right?"

"No, Cedric. We did not plan to meet here." *Although it would have been nice if we had.* "I am just as surprised to see him here as you are angry that he is here."

"So, I guess y'all gonna hang out at the fair for the rest of the night, huh?"

"No, Cedric. We talked about it just before your snitching-ass daughter called," Thalia said, looking directly at Aliza. "And we agreed that since it's going to be a problem when I get off the phone, he would say 'nice meeting you' to our children, and they go on about their business, and we go our separate ways."

"What's gonna be a problem, me?"

"Yes, Cedric, you. You're gonna be a problem. Look at you. On your snitching-ass daughter's phone, having to explain a purely innocent meeting with a client."

Cedric didn't say anything right away. "Well, I ain't gonna be no problem. If y'all wanna hang out for the rest of the night, I got no problem with that," he said, trying to be the bigger, "I'm not jealous" kind.

Thalia laughed as she watched her children and Michael's niece and nephews walking away, headed in the direction of the rides with Michael, who was looking back at Thalia as if he were asking her what he should do now that the children had gotten together.

"I don't think that could be avoided at this point since your snitching-ass daughter is giggling all up in Michael's nephew's face, about to get on a ride."

"Y'all have a good time," Cedric said and abruptly ended the call.

Therefore, when she and Michael went out to dinner the following night, there was no problem, and when she got home sometime before ten for a change, he was the one who was home, and he was sitting in the living room.

"Where've you been?" he said and sat up straight.

"Out having dinner with a client."

"Okay," he said, feeling somewhat defeated.

Consequently, when she had dinner with him the following evening, there weren't any questions. There was nothing but a good time to be had by all.

"I'm sorry about the flowers," Michael said. "I just couldn't resist the temptation."

"It's all good. I think every man needs a wakeup call every once in a while."

Chapter Twenty-two

"I would be more than happy to investigate the matter on your behalf. I'm going to transfer you to my assistant. She will take your information, and she'll be your primary contact. Hold on," Ciara said and made the transfer.

"Ciara Reynolds's office. This is Francesca Garner. How can I help you?"

"I'm getting ready to transfer a call."

"Run it."

"Hold on," she said and sent the call.

That gave her a chance to breathe. Ciara leaned back in her chair and shut her eyes. But the respite was short-lived, as her cell phone rang. She opened her desk to get her phone. Ciara looked at the display: Thalia Blackburn.

"Hey, girl."

"You got a minute to talk?"

"Sure. What's up?"

"There's this guy," Thalia began and told Ciara about Dr. Michael Wilkerson.

"What's wrong with that? Because I don't see a downside."

"The downside is that he sent two dozen roses to the office to spite Cedric."

"Here again, I'm not seeing a downside."

"I am still married to Cedric. And he works here, too."

"Okay. I can see where that might be a problem."

"Thank you."

"My advice is to deal with it when it comes up."

"It did. Remember, Cedric works here. As soon as he came through the door, his office snitch told him about the flowers, and he headed straight for my office to ask who sent those to me."

"What did you say?"

"I told him part of the truth. I said they were from him thanking me for a job well done."

"Did he go for that?"

"Yeah. Only after a bunch of questions about whether I'm fucking the good doctor. Which I'm not, so I didn't have to lie."

"He just asked the wrong question."

"That's what I thought," Thalia said and laughed.

"My advice remains the same. Deal with it when, and only when, it becomes an issue. Until then, don't worry about it."

"Easier said than done, but you're right."

"I always am."

"I'll deal with it when and if it becomes an issue." Thalia paused. "I need to take this call. Thank you."

"I'll talk to you later," Ciara said and ended the call. She leaned back in her chair and closed her eyes. Once again, her break was interrupted by Francesca calling.

"What's up?"

"Leona Chandler is in the city and would like to see you today."

Ciara shook her head. "Tell her that I am unavailable and schedule a call for tomorrow morning."

"Got you," Francesca said and went to tell Leona what Ciara said.

Some people have nerve, Ciara thought. Once again, Ciara leaned back and closed her eyes. However, what she thought about was that night in Saint Barts.

With her legs in the air, Ciara held Leona's head in place with one hand and squeezed her nipple with the other as Leona eased two fingers in and out of her wetness. Ciara squeezed her nipples harder, and Leona sucked her clit and penetrated her harder with her fingers. Ciara felt a wave rush over her entire body.

"Oh, shitttttt."

When Ciara opened her eyes from the mind-numbing orgasm Leona had given her, Tobias was seated in the chair across from them. He was naked, his dick was hard, and he was stroking it. Ciara watched as he spat in his hand before going back to stroking himself, leaving his dick glistening in the warm glow of the room.

Ciara watched him jerk off, and coupled with the sensation of Leona working magic with her tongue, it brought her to another quick but hard orgasm. Even though Ciara's body was still shaking, Leona didn't stop. She crawled on her hands and knees above Ciara and kissed her all over her body. She paused to lick and suck Ciara's nipples, and she never wanted her to stop.

Her clit was throbbing by the time she moved on to suck Ciara's neck. Then she took Ciara's nipple into her mouth and shoved Ciara's legs apart again. She slid her body between Ciara's thighs, and she felt her moist lips and clit rub against hers.

She looked over at Tobias, and as she watched him stroke himself, she slowly lifted Ciara's leg and began riding her pussy slowly, sucking on Ciara's calf, squeezing her nipple, and rocking her hips back and forth against Ciara's pussy. Ciara glanced at Tobias, his eyes were open wide, and he was stroking that fat cock faster.

"Yes, yes!" Leona screamed, and her head drifted back as Ciara rocked against her, feeling another orgasm building.

When she screamed, Tobias sprang to his feet and came toward them quickly, still stroking. Leona's body jerked and then jerked again.

"I'm cumming," she screamed, and then she hopped off Ciara so fast that she almost lost her balance. Leona moved around him and placed her ass in front of him. He pulled her hips up and thrust himself inside her.

"Yes, fuck me with that big dick," she screamed.

While Leona feasted on Ciara, still working magic with her tongue, she lay there, squeezing her nipples while getting so turned on, watching the two of them. Tobias pulled completely out of her and then slammed himself into her again.

Leona lifted her head from between Ciara's thighs long enough to say, "Yeah! Fuck that pussy!"

The feeling of Leona's tongue on Ciara's clit and the sight of Tobias thrusting in and out of her caused Ciara's body to shudder. Tobias pulled out of Leona, slapped her ass, held on to her hips, and entered her slowly again before he quickly increased his pace, pounding furiously in Leona's juicy pussy until her body started to tremble.

"Fuck me, fuck me!" Leona chanted as Tobias grabbed and squeezed her cheeks and slammed his body into her, and then he brought her to a gut-wrenching orgasm.

Ciara opened her eyes and shook her head. She wasn't about to let Tobias fuck her.

Not happening, *she thought, and as soon as Leona lifted her head, Ciara ran out of there, grabbed her bikini, and rushed to her room. Ciara locked the door in case they had ideas of coming down there to finish what Leona had started.*

All Ciara could do was shake her head at the thought of it. Francesca called and said Leona wasn't happy, but she made an appointment to speak for nine thirty tomorrow morning.

"And I have Brass Fitters on line three for you."

"Go ahead and transfer them."

"Hold on."

"Ciara Reynolds."

By the end of the day, Ciara felt used and tired. She was more than ready to call it a day and go home. On the way home, Ciara stopped to eat at her favorite restaurant, Palate Pleasures, and got her favorite chicken marsala. As she enjoyed her meal with a glass of wine, her thoughts drifted once again to that night in Saint Barts. She couldn't believe how easily she gave in to Leona's slow seduction game.

Because that's what you wanted to happen, Ciara was forced to admit to herself. She wondered if that satisfied her curiosity, or would she see Leona and further that curiosity?

"No, I don't think so. I am satisfied with that," Ciara said, but then again, she had tasted what was, until that night, the forbidden fruit. There was really no telling where that taste would lead Ciara.

She went home, took a shower, and did what she had been doing each night. Ciara selected a clip to watch, broke out Ava, and did her thing. After bringing herself to an orgasm, Ciara turned off the television and went to sleep.

The following day, Ciara went to the office, knowing that she had to talk to Leona, and she wondered what she was going to say.

"Tell her politely that you're not down," Ciara said aloud and got in the car.

When she got to her desk, Francesca said Leona hadn't called yet.

"When she calls, let me know, and then give me five minutes, and then transfer the call."

"Will do."

While she waited, Ciara busied herself with research for another client. It was after ten o'clock when Leona called.

"Are you ready for her?"

"Yeah. Give me five minutes and then send her through."

When the line went silent, Ciara thought about what she was going to say to a woman who traveled from Saint Barts to Houston to have sex with her.

"The truth," Ciara said aloud and waited for the call to be transferred. Suddenly, the phone rang.

"Ciara Reynolds."

"Good morning, Ciara. Leona Chandler here."

"Yes, Leona. What can I do for you?"

"I was in town, and I was hoping to see you."

"Can you tell me the nature of your request?" Ciara asked, attempting to sound all business.

Leona chuckled. "It's more of a personal matter."

"I see."

"Good. So, when can we get together?"

"I don't think that would be appropriate."

"You don't?" she asked in disbelief.

Leona was caught completely off guard by Ciara telling her no. First of all, people didn't tell Leona Chandler no. She was sure that her slow seduction in Saint Barts had paved the way for future encounters.

"No. I don't think that would be appropriate." Ciara paused more for effect than anything else. "What I allowed to happen was inappropriate for me to engage in as your attorney."

"I would beg to differ. But go on."

"Therefore, I don't think we should engage in that behavior again. If that is a prerequisite for being your attorney, I suggest you find another attorney."

"This is disappointing, but I understand." Leona exhaled loudly. "No. It's not a prerequisite. We still want you as our attorney," Leona said grudgingly.

Since sex was a prerequisite for Leona, Ciara's refusal was reason enough to fire her. However, Tobias said they were keeping Ciara as their attorney.

"Whether you can have sex with her is on you. It has no bearing on the business and my decision," Tobias told her before she left for Houston.

Therefore, a defeated Leona had no choice. She had to accept that Ciara Reynolds was her attorney and wouldn't be having sex with her. It was a hard pill for Leona to swallow.

"I will speak with you when I have business to discuss. Thank you for taking my call."

Ciara exhaled and placed the phone back in its cradle. At the end of the day, Ciara left her office for the night. She went out to eat on the way home at a little place she found called Fusion Spark. It was an Asian food truck, which was parked by a convenience store on her way home. They served a fusion spicy shrimp and fried Indian cheese tikka masala in creamy tomato curry that she'd become fond of, and she went home to eat. Ciara watched the news in the living room, and then she got up and headed for the shower.

When she got in bed, Ciara selected a clip from Pornhub and got Ava from the drawer. After bringing herself to a mind-numbing orgasm, she turned off the television and went to sleep. But her thoughts once again drifted to Leona and the magic she weaved between her thighs. Ciara's hand eased between her thighs, and she brought herself to orgasm.

"Damn," she said and thought about it and exploded again.

Chapter Twenty-three

On Wednesday morning, Savannah arrived in her office feeling rested and refreshed after her time in Barbados with Milo.

Once Savannah and Milo landed in Barbados, they were taken by car service to the O2 Beach Club & Spa and the luxury one-bedroom oceanfront suite that Milo had arranged. As soon as they got there, Savannah went to the sliding door and went out on the deck. She raised her arms, and her head tilted back. Milo followed her out, and he wrapped his arms around her.

"I am so glad you forced this on me." She turned into his arms and kissed him long and passionately. "Come on," Savannah said. She grabbed him by the hand and rushed into their suite.

Milo started undressing with the intended desire to make love to Savannah. She excitedly opened her suitcase and dug out the bikini she'd been dying to wear since she got it a year and a half ago when she and Greyson were talking about taking a family vacation. She found it, turned to Milo, and held it up for him to see.

"What do you think?" she asked and saw that Milo was naked and rock hard lying across the bed. "What are you doing?" Milo didn't answer. He simply pointed to his erection and smiled. Savannah chuckled and shook her head. "No, buddy. You said you wanted to go to the beach, not fly me down here to fuck." She gave him the thumb. "Come on, get your sexy ass out of the bed."

Savannah looked at his rock-hard, "ready to fuck her silly" erection, and shook her head. "I can't believe I just said that."

Milo got out of bed. "Neither can I," he said, once again pointing to his rock-hard erection, ready to fuck her silly, and shook his head. "But that is what I said."

"Right. So let's go to the beach."

Savannah watched it as it went down, shook her head, and put on her bikini.

"I can't believe I said that."

Milo got his bag and dug out his swimming trunks. "I can't believe it either," he said, putting them on and taking Savannah into his arms. "But let's go to the beach!"

She kissed him. "That is what we came here for, right?" she kind of asked, taking him by the hand and leading him to the door. "Right?" she asked again as they got to the elevator bank.

"Right." Milo took her into his arms and kissed her. "I did say that. But I was planning on doing a whole hell of a lot of the bang, bang, bang, too."

The elevator doors opened, and they got on. "And I promise you we are going to do a whole hell of a lot of the bang, bang, bang, too. But you got me all hyped about going to the beach." The doors opened, and once again, Savannah took Milo by the hand. "So, after you feed me, I am going to fuck your sexy ass within an inch of your life," she said as they got outside and could see the Caribbean Sea. "But for now, we're doing this."

Savannah was as good as her word. After they had fun on the beach, they went to Bluefin, which was a short stroll from the beach. They ate jerk pork seekers, and then they headed hurriedly to the room, and she, as promised, fucked his sexy ass within an inch of his life.

Milo grabbed and squeezed one of her cheeks as Savannah began to buck harder and harder. Milo leaned forward, grabbed Savannah by the shoulders, and began to pound furiously on that ass until her body started to tremble. Milo slowed a bit and eased in and out of her. Each time he'd smack her ass. The steady motion gave her a chance to catch herself. She separated herself from Milo and rolled over on her back.

Milo once again pushed himself inside Savannah. Milo began the same slow and steady motion, and Savannah wrapped her legs around his waist. Savannah worked her hips and inner muscles while licking his nipples. This time, it was Milo's body that began to tremble, and Savannah who was pounding her hips furiously into him until she came again.

That fond memory ended with a bang when she opened and read an email from Marilyn Proctor, an Intuitive Energy vice president. The subject line read, Possible Accounting Scandals.

"It's begun."

The email detailed concerns and warned that the debts and losses were being routed into entities formed offshore, which were not included in the company's financial statement. It also suggested that financial transactions between Intuitive Energy and related companies were used to eliminate unprofitable entities.

"I agree, Marilyn. I believe that's exactly what's going on," Savannah said aloud.

"Did you say something, Savannah?" Kiera shouted from her desk.

"Just venting to myself."

Kiera got up from her desk and went into the office with Savannah. "What are you venting about?"

"Come here and take a look," Savannah said and stood up so Kiera could sit and read the email.

"And Marilyn Proctor is a VP, right?" she asked as she read. Savannah nodded, and Kiera continued reading.

"This line caught my attention. 'It is my belief that some Energy executives were privately being encouraged to tell potential investors and current shareholders to buy the stock or hold on to their stock because the stock price would rebound and could possibly reach its high of ninety-four dollars per share.'"

"That line caught my attention too," Savannah said, and Kiera got up from her desk.

Savannah sat down.

"What are you going to do?"

"I'm going to talk to Ciara."

When Kiera went back to her office, Savannah got her cell phone from her purse and was about to call Ciara when the phone rang.

"Hello, Milo."

"Good morning, Savannah. How are you?"

"I'm doing all right this morning. What about you?"

"I'm doing great. I'm at Kennedy, waiting for them to begin boarding."

"Where are you off to this morning?"

"Richmond, Virginia, to see a woman about industrial coffee machines."

"Good luck."

"The reason for my call, other than hearing your voice, is to ask if you had any plans for the weekend."

"I have no plans. What did you have in mind?" Savannah asked excitedly.

"If you didn't have any plans, which you don't, I was thinking about coming to see you this weekend."

Savannah spun around in her chair and looked out her window. It had turned out to be the only thing she was enjoying about working there. "Like I said, I have no plans for the weekend and would be happy to see you. When were you thinking about coming?"

"I could be there Friday night."

"That works for me."

"Great. Hey, they're calling my flight. I'll call you when I land in Richmond."

"Safe travels."

"Thanks," Milo said, and he ended the call.

Savannah's next call was to Ciara.

"Ciara Reynolds."

"Hey, girl."

"Hey, Savannah. What's up?"

"We need to talk."

"Okay. I have a full day today. So just come by the house tonight. Or better yet, you could come pick me up in the limousine, and we can go out to dinner somewhere."

"What do you have a taste for?"

"I'm feeling Italian and musical."

"We can do that. I'll pick you up around seven."

"I have to tell you, while I was in Saint Barts, I had a limousine at my disposal. I see what you like. I didn't feel my driving this morning."

"I know how you feel."

"I gotta take this call."

"Go. And I'll see you tonight at seven."

Later that evening, at seven, Savannah picked up Ciara in the limo, and they went to Pasta Fresca. Over chicken scarpariello and Italian wedding risotto, Savannah allowed Ciara to read the email she received from Marilyn Proctor.

"She's a VP, right?" Ciara asked as she read.

"Yes."

"I think it's time you let my friend at the FBI make the referral to the SEC. I'll make it happen and let you know when."

"Thank you, Ciara."

When Savannah returned to work the following day, she replied to Marilyn Proctor's email.

It said, Let's have lunch today.

Marilyn replied immediately. I'm free after one this afternoon.

Savannah replied, See you in the lobby at one.

When Savannah got off her elevator, the first person she saw was Marilyn. She started to say something, but Savannah cut her off before she could say too much.

"Let's talk when we get to the restaurant."

"Oh." Marilyn nodded her head. "Right. I forgot. The walls do have ears around here," she said and kept walking to the limousine.

"Good afternoon, Ms. Ayers."

"Good afternoon, Oscar. This is Marilyn Proctor," Savannah said and got into the limousine.

"Good afternoon, Ms. Proctor."

"Hello, Oscar," she said and got into the limousine. Oscar shut the door and got in.

"Where to, Ms. Ayers?"

"Fineez." It was one of her favorite spots for lunch.

"On our way."

They made company-related small talk until they got to Fineez and were seated before Marilyn restated her concerns.

"I'm concerned . . . what am I saying? I'm afraid that the debts and losses are being routed into entities formed offshore, and those transactions are not included in the company's financial statement. I'm also afraid that financial transactions between Intuitive Energy and related companies are used to eliminate unprofitable entities."

"I agree, Marilyn. I believe that's exactly what's going on," Savannah said as their server arrived with the menus.

"Good afternoon, Ms. Ayers."

"Afternoon, Louise. I don't need a menu."

Louise laughed. "Your usual?"

"Please. But she might need a minute," she said as Marilyn feverishly scanned the menu.

"I know what I want. I'll have the five-star pomegranate scallops."

"Got it. One master chef beef Wellington and a five-star pomegranate scallops. I'll put those right in for you. What would you like to drink?"

Marilyn glanced at Savannah for cues.

"I'll have an espresso martini."

"I've never had one, but . . ." Marilyn handed Louise the menu. "But I'll try anything once. I'll have an espresso martini too."

"Got it," Louise said and went about her business.

"Alone at last," Savannah said. "Like I said, I agree. I believe that is exactly what's going on. But I've been excluded from the financial end of the business, I believe intentionally."

"I see."

"However, I am like you, aware of and share your concerns. However, I am taking steps to protect myself," Savannah said as Louise returned with their cocktails.

"Are you pressed for time today, Ms. Avery?"

"Not today, Louise. Today, I am enjoying a leisurely meal with Marilyn."

Louise pointed. "Got ya," she said and left the table.

"I take it you come here often."

"I do. I love the food here. It's one of my favorite places."

"Okay. I'll see how I like the food, and if I like it, I'll add it to my list of premium lunch spots."

"I think you'll like it." Savannah sipped her drink. "But like I said, I am taking steps to protect myself, and I strongly suggest you do the same. But I was cautioned not to engage outside counsel or put an attorney on retainer."

"By whom, if you don't mind me asking and if you can say?"

"Fatima Camacho from the legal department."

"I know Fatima—"

"And you're wondering why you didn't get such a warning?"

"In fact, I am."

"She was informing me about Kiran Caldwell. She is going to be sentenced today for criminal insider trading, and I was asking what my response should be," Savannah said.

"I see," Marilyn said, nodding her head as their meal for the afternoon arrived and was served.

"When I take my next steps, I plan on mentioning you, so be prepared."

"I understand. Can you tell me what those next steps are going to be?"

"No, I'm sorry, but at this point, I cannot."

"I understand."

"But once I've taken those steps, I will inform you."

"If that's the best you can offer, I accept that." Marilyn leaned forward and whispered, "I understand the position all this nonsense puts you in, both personally and professionally."

"Thank you," Savannah said. "I didn't want you to think I was withholding important information from you just because."

"No. I completely understand." Marilyn looked around the crowded restaurant. "With you being president of a company involved in practices like this, it could ruin your reputation for years to come. So I understand your need to protect yourself."

"My official response to your email, should it come up in the future, and I'm sure it will, is that you expressed your concerns to me, and I advised you to share your concerns with your direct supervisor."

"I understand. Thank you."

Savannah picked up and unwrapped her silverware. "Now, let's eat this delicious meal."

"Right. Enough shop talk for the day," Marilyn said, unwrapping her silverware, and they ate lunch. After that, Savannah and Marilyn returned to the office.

Chapter Twenty-four

The day that Savannah had been waiting weeks for had finally come. She'd been copying files to give to the SEC and taking notes after meetings to document what was said. Savannah understood clearly that it was important to protect herself. That day, she was meeting with representatives of the Securities and Exchange Commission to talk about her knowledge of the activities going on at Intuitive Energy. Since Savannah wasn't comfortable going to the office of the Securities and Exchange Commission's regional office in Fort Worth, and their coming to Intuitive Energy was out of the question, it was decided that it would be off-site.

That morning, Debra Owsley and her associate, Paige Cox, flew in from Washington, DC. They checked into the Post Oak Hotel at Uptown Houston for a three o'clock meeting with Savannah Ayers, the president of Intuitive Energy, as well as her personal attorney and her accounting advisor. Once Savannah arrived in the suite, introductions were made, and then Debra had a request.

"Is it all right if we talk outside on the deck? It is such a beautiful day, and we have to fly back to dark, dreary DC tonight."

"Not a problem," Savannah said. "I hate being stuck inside on dark and dreary days."

"Can I get you ladies anything? Coffee, tea, water?" Paige stood up to ask.

"Thank you," Savannah said. "Some water would be nice."

"I'll have some water too," Ciara said.

"I'll have some coffee," Thalia said.

"Come on inside, Mrs. Blackburn. The coffee, cream, and sugar are inside," Paige said.

"Would you mind bringing me a bottle of water, too, please?" Debra requested.

"Not a problem," Paige said, and once Thalia stood up, she led her inside to show her where the coffee was and to get water. When they returned, they got started.

"As I said earlier, my name is Debra Owsley, and I'm an enforcement specialist at the SEC." Debra laughed. "I used to say that we are not in any way affiliated with Southeast Conference sports."

"I can see how that mistake comes up a lot," Savannah commented.

"Anyway," Debra began. "Now, I simply keep it moving, and I get right into explaining that the U.S. Securities and Exchange Commission has an enforcement division that assists in executing its law enforcement function by recommending investigations of securities law violations. That is accomplished when the commission brings civil actions in federal court or before an administrative law judge, and by prosecuting these cases on behalf of the commission."

"That's interesting," Ciara said.

"What's that, Ms. Reynolds?"

"It's nothing." She smiled. "But Jared Clarke of the FBI, who referred me to you, gave us the impression that if criminal charges were to come of this action, the FBI would step in and prosecute," Ciara said, and Savannah, as did Thalia, nodded in agreement.

"The civil enforcement authority works closely with law enforcement agencies around the U.S. and the world to bring criminal cases when appropriate. I don't know if you know this about the FBI, but they are not above big footing a case."

Savannah glanced at Ciara and Thalia. They didn't know that either.

"They like to let you do the heavy lifting, and then they jump in and do a major press conference to announce their investigation."

"I did not know that about the FBI," Ciara said.

"All SEC investigations are conducted privately, much in the manner that you conduct an audit, Mrs. Blackburn."

"I was just thinking that very same thing."

"Facts are gathered by interviewing appropriate witnesses, examining their records, reviewing data, and other methods used. With a formal order of investigation, our staff can compel witnesses via the use of subpoenas to testify, produce books, records, and other relevant documents."

"That is my process to the letter," Thalia said proudly.

"What happens then?" Ciara inquired.

"Following the investigation, our staff presents its findings to the commission to be reviewed. The commission can file a case in federal court or bring an administrative action."

"How does that work?" Savannah asked, and Ciara glanced at her.

"Whether the commission brings a case in federal court or within the SEC before an administrative law judge would, at that point, depend upon various other factors."

"What if it's both?" Thalia asked.

"When the misconduct warrants it, the commission can and most certainly will bring both proceedings."

"What will those proceedings look like?" Ciara asked.

"A complaint filed with a U.S. district court. Our staff will ask the court for an injunction, which can also require audits, accounting for fraud, or special supervisory arrangements."

"So, what you're saying is that if an injunction is filed, the SEC can place a monitor at Intuitive Energy?" Savannah asked, and once again Ciara gave her the look.

"Yes, Ms. Ayers. We can and will. It prohibits any further acts or practices that violate the law or commission rules. We have a lot of tools in the toolbox, I assure you."

"Of this, I had no doubt," Ciara said.

"If you have what my good friend Jared Clarke says you have, the SEC can seek disgorgement."

"What's that?" Savannah asked.

"Civil monetary penalties or the return of illegal profits. The court may also have the power to bar or suspend any individual from serving as a corporate officer or director."

Savannah leaned closer to Ciara. "What if it's an administrative action?" she asked because, to this point, Savannah hadn't heard anything that protected her.

"What if the commission finds it more of an administrative action? Will you seek a variety of sanctions through the administrative proceeding process?" Ciara asked on Savannah's behalf. She was glad that Savannah had remembered the plan and would hopefully let her ask the questions from here on.

"Excellent question, Ms. Reynolds. They differ from civil court actions in that they are heard by an administrative law judge, or ALJ, who works independently of the commission. The ALJ is a law judge who directs the hearing and considers the evidence represented by our staff. I think now would be a good time for us to have a look at your documentation," Debra requested.

Savannah glanced at Ciara, and she opened her satchel and removed the documents Savannah had. Due to their sensitive nature, it was decided that the documents weren't safe for Savannah being on the premises; therefore, the documentation was given to Ciara.

"This is what we have," she said, and Ciara handed Debra the documents she received from Savannah and then she smiled. "I took the liberty and printed two copies of each document."

"Thank you, Ms. Reynolds. It was as if you knew there would be two of us performing this interview," Debra said, and she handed Paige the copy. As the ladies read what Savannah provided, she, Ciara, and Thalia whispered among themselves.

That was until Debra glanced at Paige, and she glanced at Debra.

"Wow," Debra said of the documents that quite clearly implicated the Intuitive Energy board members in a systemic fraud scheme that had cost their investors millions of dollars.

"I'm saying," Paige said and went back to reading the documents. She looked up at Savannah. "This is the mother lode, Debra."

"Yes, Paige," she said without looking up from the documents she was reading. "We got something serious here."

Ciara held up her hand, and she and Savannah fist bumped.

"Y'all brought the funk," Thalia whispered.

"They did," Debra said without looking up from the documents she was reading. "They put the serious funk back in it."

Thalia fist bumped Ciara and Savannah.

"What happens now?" Ciara asked.

"We're going to have some questions about how these documents were obtained," Paige said when Debra didn't answer the question.

"Once we're finished reading them, of course," Debra said once again without looking away from the document she was reading.

"I could answer that question for you now," Savannah said quickly because she was in a hurry to get this over with as soon as possible. Debra held her hand and finally looked up.

"Now, how were these obtained, Ms. Avery?"

"The email was received, as it says, from Marilyn Proctor, a VP at Intuitive Energy. The rest of the documentation was received from my contact in the IT department. He showed me how to download them."

"Good that you performed the download yourself for the chain of custody issues," Paige said when she finally finished reading and looked up.

"Thank you," Savannah said. "My guy was more concerned about his job for obvious reasons. So, when he left my office, I performed the download," Savannah said and once again fist bumped with Ciara.

"What happens now?" Ciara asked again.

"We'll take them back to the office and review them once again," Paige began. "And we'll open an investigation into the goings-on at Intuitive Energy."

"I think we have all that we're going to need from you, Ms. Avery," Debra said and stood up. "You are free to go if you like."

Savannah was the first to stand. She looked at Ciara and Thalia. "Thank you for your time and attention," she said and started for the door.

"Thank you, ladies," she said, and her girls stood up and followed Savannah to the door.

"Thank you for coming and providing us with this documentation. It is going to be quite explosive when it is explored."

It was the documentation that told the story.

"Thank you," Savannah said and opened the door to the suite.

Chapter Twenty-five

Thalia had thought long and hard about this, and although she made her decision, she was happy about it. She just wanted to be reassured that she was doing the right thing.

"You're planning on staying with Cedric for the sake of the children."

"Don't you think I have to?"

"No, Thalia, I don't. Cedric is a fucking asshole who cheats on you constantly. No, Thalia, I don't think you should stay with him."

"Don't you think I have to for my children?"

When she put it that way, Thalia was right. Therefore, despite her feelings that Cedric was an asshole, who was often rude to her, Ciara knew it was her responsibility to support her bestie. She knew that those kids were her heart and soul.

"When you put it that way, you're right. So, despite my feeling that Cedric is an asshole who doesn't deserve a great woman like you, you need to stay for the kids."

"I always am right," Thalia said proudly.

"I know those kids are your world."

"They are."

"And that is the only reason I think you should stay with the asshole, for the children."

"They need their father. And, despite him being an asshole who cheats on me constantly, I do love him. And that is the only reason I'm staying with him, for my children. I can get a man," Thalia said.

“The fact is that you did that. You found a man. You found a man who obviously adores you.”

“He does. And that’s another reason I need to end it with Michael. He does adore me.”

“See there. But you’re right. You need to be a woman who is about your children.”

“It would be a nice change from women these days who are all about themselves. Fuck their kids, it’s all about them.”

“You’re right.”

“Like I said, sister girl, I always am. And I think Savannah would agree with me,” Thalia chuckled. “That is if I could ever get her to answer the phone.”

“You know she’s sweating the whole Securities and Exchange Commission thing. Maybe you should cut her some slack.”

“Maybe. But I’m used to getting her to call me back when I leave a message. But you’re right—”

“I always am,” Ciara said proudly. “Look at the time, girl. I need to go. Cut Savannah some slack,” she said.

“I know she deserves it. Do you think she’ll have a problem with them?”

“What do you mean, problems?”

She can be so precise when an answer is right in front of her, she thought but kept it to herself. *But she is a lawyer, so she has to be precise in everything she does.*

“Do you think that the Securities and Exchange Commission will investigate and indict Savannah for the crimes committed by her board of directors?”

“No. Why would they indict Savannah? She is the whistleblower. She’ll be all right in this.”

“I’m just making sure. You know how funky our government can be when it comes to us,” Thalia said, and she thought about wiretapping phones and the NSA.

"I hope not," Ciara said, and then she thought about it. "Facts. But I think our girl will be all right. Like I said, she's the whistleblower. They generally don't mess with them. If she committed any crimes, she'll get a slap on the wrist for it."

"Just making sure. You know, since our names are attached to hers and with how our fucked-up-ass government is now."

Thalia did have a point, as she thought about how fucked up the government was now. "No, I don't think so."

"At least, I hope not." Ciara laughed loud and hearty. "I am her attorney of record. In some countries, I would be going to jail right along with her."

Thalia laughed. "What countries are those so I can avoid them?"

"You silly."

"I know. Now, let's get back to my issue with Michael please. You really think I should tell Michael I'm staying with Cedric for the sake of my children?"

"Yes, girl. You know your children come first in your book."

"Nothing comes before my babies."

"Right," Ciara said reluctantly, but she said it anyway and with feeling so Thalia would think she meant it. "That means you have no choice. Those kids mean everything to you. You have got to cut everything for them."

"See, I knew I was right. Thank you, Ciara. I love you and Savannah. You two always give the best advice," Thalia said. "I'm going to go and handle my business," she said.

"It's your business, handle it. Bye," Ciara said and ended the call.

Now that she had made her decision, it was simply a matter of telling Michael. That was going to be a lot harder than it sounded. He had announced his intention to make Thalia his woman. He knew that she had been cheated on by her husband, and he promised never to do anything close to that. He said the energy that he felt the first time he saw her prevented him from doing anything that would hurt her.

"I feel so much for you at this point that I couldn't, wouldn't, do anything close to that ever."

As she had many times before, Thalia thought about leaving Cedric. However, there were the children she had to think about. He was a great father, and he loved his children. She knew that breaking up that relationship would have a long-lasting effect on the children.

Then there was their partnership in Levanter Auditoria. Dividing that business would be a nightmare. At the time, that made Cedric cheaper to keep. But now, Thalia had a chance at real happiness. Was she willing to throw him away because he was and had been a cheater? Was she ready to throw that opportunity away? Was she ready to give that opportunity up for her children?

The answer was yes, of course, she was ready. Thalia had been ready to go for years.

Now, Michael would have a chance to back up his words with action. But Thalia was going to deny him that chance. Her decision would mean that she wouldn't have a chance at real happiness. She would remain stuck in a marriage to a man who cheated on her constantly and then came home hard and ready to fuck her. Thalia would do anything for her children.

"For my children, it would be worth it."

All she had to do now was tell Michael that he was but he also wasn't her choice for a long-term mate. When she hung up the phone with Ciara, Thalia stood up and closed her office door because Cedric was in the office early for some reason. Then she sat down and called Michael.

"Can you meet me at Ocean Essence?"

"Of course I can," he said and chuckled. "Wouldn't you rather I come pick you up?"

"No, Michael, I don't want"—*or frankly need,* she said to herself—"you to come pick me up."

Michael, once again, chuckled confidently. "All right, I'll meet you at Ocean Essence. What time?"

"Say six?"

"See you at six at Ocean Essence."

After she ended the call with Michael, Thalia got her purse from the drawer and left the office. It was three in the afternoon, and the children would be home by three thirty. Therefore, she was there when they got there.

"You're home, Mommy. What's wrong?" Aliza asked.

"Nothing is wrong. I just needed to talk to you."

"What's up, Mommy?" Eric asked.

"I said nothing was wrong. I just need to talk to your sister." She looked at Aliza. "Come on."

She left the living room, leaving Eric and Sylvie to wonder what was going on because their mother never came home early unless there was a damn good reason.

Thalia led Aliza to her home office and closed the door. At that point, Aliza began to wonder what was wrong or what she had done.

"Sit down."

"Now you're scaring me, Mommy. What's wrong?" she asked and sat down as her mother asked.

"What's wrong is that I've been seeing a man." Thalia saw the look on Aliza's face and held up her hand. "No, I didn't have sex with him," she said honestly because she was only talking about her relationship with Michael and not Griffin. "We've gone out a few times, and I like him. I mean, I really like him, but I am on my way to tell him that I can't see him anymore because of you children. I wanted to ask you what you thought of it."

"You're talking about leaving Daddy?"

"Yes."

"Why would you want to leave Daddy?"

She paused before answering and thought carefully about what she was going to tell her daughter about her father. She exhaled. "Your father cheats on me and has for years."

"Daddy?"

"Anytime your father stays out until ten, he's with another woman."

Aliza got an indignant look on her face. "Why do you stay with him?"

"I love your father, and I stay because of you children."

"I understand."

"I need to know what you thought before I went and ended it with him."

Aliza stood up and began pacing in the small office. "I don't know what to tell you, Mommy."

"I would be divorcing your father."

"I understand that and I understand why. But you would be divorcing Daddy. Would you be getting married again and moving in with the other man? What is his name anyway?"

"His name is Michael. And no, I wouldn't be getting married and moving him into our house. But I still want to know what you think."

"Why me?"

"Because you're the oldest." She smiled. "And you're my mini me."

Aliza smiled because she knew, in so many ways, she really was her mother's mini me. "I get that, I do, but you're asking me to decide whether to leave Daddy. That's a lot of pressure."

"I just wanna know what you think. Don't get it twisted. I just need to know what you would think if that were to happen."

Aliza sat down and looked at her mother. "I think you should give Daddy another chance."

"I've given him another chance for years. But you answered my question."

"What are you gonna do?"

"I don't know yet," she lied because Thalia knew exactly what she was going to do when she got to Ocean Essence.

When Thalia went to open the door, Aliza stood up and followed her out of the office.

"I'll be back. I won't be long," Thalia said and hoped she was right. She opened the door. "If your father just happens to come home, tell him I'll be home soon."

Thalia left the house and headed for Ocean Essence with the confidence that she was going to do the right thing for everybody but her. She had gotten to the restaurant early because she needed a drink or two for what she was about to do for her children. At five thirty, Michaell walked in, saw her, and bypassed the hostess station.

"I see my party," he said and came straight for the table.

Thalia took a deep breath. "Thank you for coming."

Michael sat down and once again chuckled confidently. "Why wouldn't I? I would do anything you asked me to do."

"I have something that I need to tell you."

Michael looked around the crowded restaurant. "We need a server. I'm starving."

"I need for you to hear what I have to say."

"This sounds serious," Michael said, and the confident chuckling was gone.

"It is."

"What's up?"

Thalia took a deep breath. "I've decided to stay with my husband."

"Why? If he cheats on you, he can't really love you the way you should be loved."

"I know."

"I would treat you like the queen you are."

"And I know you would. But I'm not doing this for me."

"This is about your children, isn't it?"

"It is. I would do anything for my children, and yes, that includes staying with my husband. Who cheats on me and can't really love me the way I should be loved. I know that you would love and cherish me like the queen I am, but I can't take their father from them. Yes, I understand what that means for me. I would have to continue to endure his constant cheating, and I am willing to do it because I can't take their father away from them."

Michael looked shocked by what he was hearing. The smile was gone and was replaced by a frown that would have, not long ago, broken Thalia's will.

"I understand." He nodded. "But I can't be your outside man. I just won't do that."

Thalia nodded. "I understand. And I want you to know this really breaks my heart to have to tell you this, but I have to do what's right for my children."

"And I understand that. I really do and I do understand that you have to do what's right for your children." Michael exhaled. "I just wasn't expecting this." He shook his head. "Not in a million years, I didn't expect this."

"I'm sorry."

Michael reached across the table and took her hand in his. "Don't be. You're doing what's right for your children. I completely understand that. I just can't be a part of it."

"I know, and I completely understand it." Thalia let out a little laugh. "And that's why it breaks my heart to do this."

"And I understand that." Michael laughed out loud, and Thalia wondered why. "We sure are doing a lot of understanding for something, to be honest with you, I don't think either of us wants or truly understands, but it is the right thing to do."

She squeezed his hand. "Thank you for understanding."

"You didn't hear me say neither of us truly understands?"

"I did. And you're right. I don't understand it, but here I am doing it."

Michael pointed to the empty drink glass on the table. "At least you had a drink to do this." He chuckled. "I had to hear this and get my heart broken sober."

Thalia raised her hand for a waitress.

"What can I do for you?"

"We'd like to order cocktails."

"What can I bring for you, sir?"

"Ketel One and orange juice, please."

She turned to Thalia. "Another vodka tonic?"

"Please."

"Coming right up," she said and left the table.

There wasn't much conversation until she returned with the drinks.

"Here you go." She placed the check on the table. "I'll take that whenever you're ready," she said and left the table.

Michael raised his glass. "To doing what's right and not what we want," he said and drained the glass. "I should have told the waitress not to go far," he said and looked for her. "I'm gonna need another drink behind this," he said and raised his hand.

"It works better if I do it," Thalia said, and she raised her hand.

A waitress came right to the table. "What can I get for you?"

"He's gonna need another."

"Leaving so soon?" Michael asked.

"I think I wore out my welcome after what I just dropped on you."

"You did, but I'm feeling benevolent," he said, and he chuckled. "So I'm sitting here having a drink with the woman I thought I was in love with—"

"Don't do that."

"What?"

"Play with my heart like that," she said as the drinks arrived.

"I wasn't. Really."

"Okay. But I really should go." Thalia gathered her things and shot her drink. "To the relationship I wanted." Thalia stood up. "Goodbye, Michael."

Thalia left the restaurant in tears over what she had just done. When she got home, of course, Cedric wasn't there and hadn't been. She hugged her children when she got there. Eric and Sylvie wondered why she had tears in her eyes, but Aliza understood, and she cried along with her mother for what she knew she had done for them.

Chapter Twenty-six

For most people and most lawyers, this would have been a busy, drama-filled day. But not for Ciara. To her, when seven o'clock came, she knew it was just another day in the life of Ciara Reynolds.

"Ciara Reynolds, superstar."

Ciara turned off her laptop, unplugged it, and put it in the Maison de Sabre leather laptop bag that Zack got her.

"I really should have tossed that with the rest of the stuff he bought me." But Ciara loved that bag, so she was keeping it. Once she had packed up, she headed for the elevator. When she got into the parking garage and approached her car, she saw somebody leaning on the car next to it. The closer Ciara got, the more she knew she didn't want to have this conversation. But at this point, it was inevitable.

"What could you possibly want, Zack?"

He looked the same, handsome and confident, but Ciara had known him long enough to see the cracks in his once well-polished armor.

"I thought you might have calmed down by now and you might be willing to hear me out."

Although she wanted to scream, Ciara refused to give him that satisfaction. Although it was over between them, it was still very much a battle of wills.

"Yes. I have 'calmed down.'" Ciara used air quotes. "But it hasn't left me any more inclined to hear anything your butt-fucking ass has to say to me."

***

Zack wanted her to stop calling him that, but he knew after what she saw him doing, the title "butt-fucking ass" was appropriate. He had always been able to manipulate Ciara into doing what he wanted her to do. But not this time. This time, she wasn't going to be weak.

"Please, Ciara, just hear me out, and if you still feel the same way, I'll leave and you'll never see or hear from me again."

Ciara reached into her purse and took out the can of pepper spray. "Get the fuck away from me, or I swear, Zack, I will pepper spray your butt-fucking ass and start screaming. The guard at the gate will hear me from here, lock down this garage because he's looking for some action, and come running."

Zack didn't seem to care. He went into what he had to say. When Ciara sprayed him, he knew it was coming, so he was able to dodge it and went into what he came to say. When she started screaming, he was undeterred.

"It was only that one time—"

"Bullshit."

"It's not bullshit," he lied. "It was just the one time."

"Whatever. Say what you think you need to say so you can take your butt-fuckin' ass on away from me."

"I still think we can make our thing work."

"How? You fuck men in the ass. I'm dying to hear, how do you think we can still make it work?"

"Okay, it's true, I am what you say I am—"

"A butt fucker."

"Yes. But I have been the entire time you've known me."

"I figured as much."

"And before a month ago, you were dying to marry me."

"That was before I knew that you were a butt fucker."

"We can still get married. We don't have to have sex. You can have your own room in our house. I know you've probably told everybody—"

"No, I haven't. Just my girls. I was too ashamed to tell anybody else. And believe me, if I wasn't so ashamed that I was engaged to a gay man, I would have blown up your entire world. Everyone would know that you're a closeted gay man."

"We can do this."

"No, Zack, we can't. I wouldn't marry you now for a million dollars."

"I understand," Zack said, and he walked to his car and got in. Although he was glad that Ciara wasn't going to blow up his world and tell everyone that he was gay, he really thought there was a chance, albeit a slim one, that he and Ciara Reynolds could be married and be somewhat happy together. He drove away knowing that wasn't going to be.

Ciara stood and watched until Zack had driven out of the parking lot before she got in the car. She unlocked her car and got in. She breathed a sigh of relief and went home.

When she got there, she felt like hanging out, so she jumped in the shower. When she got out, Ciara fought the urge to lie down and masturbate, went into her closet, and got dressed. She went to her new favorite spot, Mentara.

Once inside, it wasn't long before someone was in her face with a rap she was digging. But he got a text message, and he apologized and ran outta there so fast it made her head spin. Ciara laughed, shook her head, and waited for the next man to come and sit down.

When one did, he had more of a rap to put on her. She wasn't as impressed with him as the last one, but she sat there and acted like she was into what he was saying. They danced once, and then the club was closed for happy hour, and then it started to get crowded.

When Ciara saw it was about to get crowded, she told her newest suitor she was leaving and got his number in case she ever decided to call him, and she went home. After another shower, Ciara did what she had done lately when she showered and got in bed. Ciara broke out Ava, and she did what she did. Once she had a screaming orgasm, she turned off the television to go to sleep. As she lay there, Ciara had an epiphany.

"You don't need to have a man," Ciara said aloud. "I can just date whoever steps to me and keep it moving."

With that simple revelation, Ciara decided to live the single life for a while. That would give her the opportunity to find out who Ciara Reynolds was post Zack. She lay there for a minute or two thinking about what a single Ciara Reynolds life would look like, and she laughed.

"I'll be a dating thug," Ciara shouted, pumped her fist, rolled over, and went to sleep.

The next morning, Ciara woke up happy and with a new attitude. After a long, hot shower, Ciara went into her dressing room and picked out a cream Khaite Winona layered shift minidress that she wore with Stuart Weitzman leather d'Orsay pumps. She completed the outfit with a pair of Dolce & Gabbana goldstone pearl monogram heart drop earrings. On the way out the door, Ciara grabbed her Maison de Sabre leather laptop bag and headed for the office.

It was just another day at the office for Ciara. The usual meetings with paralegals in advance of consultation with clients, looking over briefs, nothing out of the ordinary. It was getting late on a Friday afternoon, and Ciara began getting ready to leave. Now that she was a "dating thug," she was thinking about what she was going to do for the weekend.

Ciara dropped the laptop in the bag and headed for the elevator. When she was almost there, her phone began ringing. She reached into her bag and glanced at the display to see who was calling.

"Jared Clarke," she answered. "How've you been?"

"I've been doing fine, beautiful Ciara. How have you been doing?"

"I am awesome," she said as the elevator came and she got on. "What about you? It's been a minute since we've talked. What's going on in your world?"

"Well, let me see. The last time we talked, you said you needed to, how did you put it, go on a mission of rediscovery. How's that going, by the way?"

"It's a work in progress."

"Anyway, I got the impression that you needed space to complete your mission of rediscovery."

"And?"

"And I thought I was too late, bad timing, whatever you wanna call it. I had missed my opportunity again."

"You know, old Ciara would've had to play coy and say something flirtatious, but as part of that mission of rediscovery, I've decided to, you know, cut through the bullshit. You know what I mean?"

"I do."

"Good." The elevator doors opened, and Ciara walked into the parking garage to her car. "So, I'm going to just go ahead and tell you that when I told you about my mission of rediscovery, I had a part for you to play in that rediscovery."

"Oh."

"Yeah, oh. So, let's do this. I take it you're free this evening?" she asked and unlocked her car.

Jared chuckled. "I am free this evening."

"I figured that's why you called." Ciara laughed lightly. "You probably said, 'I don't have anything to do tonight. Let me see what's up with Ciara and her mission of rediscovery.'"

"Keeping it real, aren't you?"

Ciara got in and started the car. "In this mission of rediscovery, ain't no other way to be." She laughed. "My mother used to play this record by a group called First Choice. They had this song 'Runnin' Out of Fools.' So, I guess you got back to my name in your little black book," she laughed.

"I assure you I don't have a little black book."

"I know that. So, let's do this. To make up for the misunderstanding, since you're not doing anything tonight, meet me at the Thai Front. You know where that is?"

"Google does. What time?"

"I'm getting ready to go to the gym. Is eight o'clock too late for you?"

"Not at all. I will see you at eight o'clock when Google tells me how to get to the Thai Front."

"It's around the Kemah Boardwalk. I'll see you there," Ciara said.

"Oh, yeah. I almost forgot the reason that I called."

"I tend to do that to men."

"You might want to mention to Savannah that the SEC is going to hold a press conference soon about Intuitive Energy."

"I'll give her a call and let her know to expect it."

After a good workout at the gym, Ciara got to the Thai Front at a quarter to eight and allowed the hostess to seat Jared when he got there. The hostess escorted him to the table and pulled out his chair to sit down.

"Good evening, beautiful Ciara."

"Hello, Jared. You know, every time I see you, I forget how fine you are."

"Thank you," Jared said. "You're spitting it rough, rugged, and raw, ain't you?"

"In this mission of rediscovery, there ain't no other way to be," Ciara said as their server arrived at the table.

"Are you ready to order?"

"I'd like to see the menu first."

"Here you go," the server said, and she handed Jared a menu.

Ciara ordered the pad Thai, and Jared got the khao pad with chicken and shrimp. As it was the last time they shared a meal, Ciara and Jared had a lively conversation where they found that they had so much to talk about. At the conclusion of their meal, Ciara was enjoying the conversation and his company so much that she wanted to keep talking to him. So, Ciara and Jared walked along the Kemah Boardwalk and talked.

"Tell me your story, Mr. Jared Clarke."

"What do you want to know?"

"What do you want me to know? Let's start with the day we met. You asked me to dinner, but I had just gotten engaged, so I declined the invitation."

"Okay."

"What were you doing in between then and the time you walked your sexy ass into Euphoria Elixirs to talk to Savannah?"

"To be honest with you—"

"There ain't no other way to be."

"I was dating different women." They walked in silence for a few seconds. "You see, I haven't found anybody I'd really want to be in any kind of relationship with." Jared shook his head. "I'll be honest, and I know there ain't no other way to be, but the pickings are slim out there."

"Tell me about it. But you're right. The pickings are slim out there."

Once again, there was silence as they walked. Then Ciara said, "For some reason, I feel comfortable talking to you. I haven't decided whether that is a good or a bad thing, but it's a thing. Anyway, that's kind of where I am in my mission of rediscovery. I met the last guy, and six months later, I was calling myself engaged to Mr. Butt Fucker."

"At least you have a good attitude about it."

"My daddy used to say, like the prophet James Brown said, it is what it is. Might as well deal with it."

"That is still an enlightened attitude to have."

"It is what it is. But my point is, that time, I rushed in and allowed myself to get caught up in his world. It was always about what he wanted to do. That time with him changed me. Changed who I am."

"How so?"

Ciara smiled. "Let's say there have been some changes in my sexuality as a result of my association with him."

"Now I'm intrigued."

"Understandable. Anytime a woman mentions anything about her sexuality, men are intrigued."

Jared laughed. "Still spitting it rough, rugged, and raw."

"I told you, there ain't no other way to be."

"I can handle it. Bring it on."

"And I like you, FBI Agent Jared Clarke."

"Do you?"

"I really do. Anyway, I'm not going to rush into a relationship just for the sake of saying I got a man."

"I know what you mean."

"So last night, I declared myself a dating thug."

Jared laughed. "A dating thug."

Ciara nodded. "That's right, a dating thug."

"What does being a dating thug even look like?"

"I don't know. But what I do know is . . . how did you put it? I want you to be a part of my rediscovery. I'm not trying to get all hooked up because I'm a thug, but I'd like to see more of you. You think you can do that with me?"

"I think I can. I can be a dating thug with you, beautiful Ciara."

Chapter Twenty-seven

Savannah was alone and the fact of the matter was she hated being alone. She wandered around the house looking for something, anything, to do, but there was nothing. When the doorbell rang, Savannah rushed to open it. And there was a package on the ground. She took the package into the house. It was from Milo. Savannah opened the box, and she found another box. Savannah opened that box only to find another box. She opened that one, and you guessed it, another box. She opened that box. It had a note in that box. Savannah ripped open the envelope and read the handwritten note.

Hey, Savannah,
I got some time off.
Can I come to see you?

Savannah dropped the paper on the ground and called Milo right away. What she got was his voicemail.

"Damn it!" Savannah shouted. "I got his voicemail." She left a message. "It's Savannah. Why did you send me that note and not be around to take my call? Please call me when you get this. Please." She ended the call and hung up.

Just then, the phone rang again, this time with a call from Ciara. However, by the time Savannah made it to the phone, Ciara had gone to voicemail, and she hung up.

She called Ciara back to see what she wanted. "Another one. Black people," she said. "I am sick of voicemail. Call me back, please."

When she finished calling Ciara, Savannah called Milo again and once again got his voicemail. After she left him an angry voicemail, the doorbell rang. Savannah glanced at her watch. It was too late for regular mail, so maybe it was UPS or FedEx. She walked to the door, thinking that it would be funny if it was her ex-husband, Greyson, who was the driver making the delivery. Savannah took her time getting to the door. However, when she finally made it to the door and opened it, she was shocked to see Milo standing there.

"Hi."

"Get in here."

Savannah pulled him into the house, and suddenly she was all lips and hands all over his body. The way she was kissing him, it wouldn't be long before they were naked and engaged in sex. They made it as far as the living room. Then their clothes were off, and he entered her with force.

Milo placed kisses along her thighs, to her stomach, and then to her lips. When he used his tongue on her the way he did, opening up her wet lips and painting circles around the most sensitive part of her, Savannah screamed and came so hard that her toes curled.

Savannah felt her body tremble as Milo spread her lips, slid his tongue inside her, and then he sucked her lips, and then he sucked and licked her button with the tip of his tongue. Savannah looked down at Milo between her thighs, making her quiver in ecstasy with his finger and his tongue.

He flipped Savannah over, got to his knees, grabbed her ass, and smacked each cheek once.

Savannah felt exhilarated by his stiff length inside her, and she ground her hips into his with each deep stroke. The feeling for Savannah was so intense that her warmth immediately tightened around him. Milo began to pump it to her harder, sliding in and out of her, making Savannah eager for more. He slid his hands along her back and up her shoulders, and then he went back to his slow, steady pace. Savannah moved her hips harder and faster, trying to hold on to that feeling for just a little longer.

Savannah looked over her shoulder. His eyes were closed, and the look on his face could only be described as contentment. And she was right. It felt so wonderful being inside Savannah. The way Milo was hitting her spot was mind-blowing. It made Savannah start throwing her body at him, making him go faster, to move deeper in and out of her, and to slam it in her harder. Milo ground her hips and spanked her ass lightly. Milo felt her tightening around him, and he reached for her shoulders and pounded his length into her. The way he was making love to her, lazy and then intense, was driving her insane.

Savannah took a deep breath and looked at Milo. His thighs slapped against hers, and the heaviness of his now taut balls smacked her sensitive bud, making her orgasm inevitable. And when he took to holding both hips to get her spot the way she liked it, he felt her tighten and then spasm around him. Savannah screamed Milo's name as she surrendered to the weight of the intense climax.

"This was a nice surprise. Thank you. I need this today."

"Just today?"

Savannah let out a little laugh. "I need you every day. But for some reason, today was different. I just felt so alone in this house."

"I thought you were getting used to being alone."

"I am. But like I said, today was different." Savannah took a playful swing at Milo. "And you didn't help matters, you playing with me the way you did."

"I thought it was kind of romantic."

"Don't get me wrong, it was romantic, and it was a wonderful surprise. I just hated calling you and leaving messages for you. But the box in a box," Savannah said, pointing at him. "That was inspired."

"I'm glad you liked it."

"So, how long do I have the pleasure of your company?"

"How long do you want me?"

"All the time. I want you all the time."

"Let me ask you a question."

"Shoot."

"Suppose I were to move to Houston?"

"Is that a possibility?"

"I have an interview with a company called Insight Innovators. They're based here in Houston. You heard of them?"

"No, I haven't." Savannah got out of bed, got her tablet, and came back to bed. "You said Insight Innovators, right?"

"Right. They sell ergonomic chairs and, get this, they sell hammock chairs."

Savannah found the company website. "It looks like a good company, but it is their company website. They're supposed to put their best foot forward. You think you can sell ergonomic and hammock chairs?"

"I can sell anything."

"I would love it if you got the job and moved here." Savannah paused because she didn't want to assume too much. "If you were to move to Houston, would you buy a house or a condo, or would you get an apartment?"

"Well, let's talk about that."

"Let's." Savannah propped a pillow up behind her head. Milo laid his head across her lap.

"If I were to move to Houston, where would you want me to live?"

"The part of me that hates being alone in this house wants you to stay here with me. But on the other hand, there's a part of me, the logical part of me, telling me that if you did move here, you should get an apartment first."

"If that's what you want, then that's what we'll do."

"You sure?"

"Yes, I'm sure. This is your town, and I'm invading it. We'll do whatever you think is best. I'll look for one of those corporate apartments and get a six-month lease."

"Because you have a house full of furniture, don't you?"

"That's no problem. I can put my stuff in storage until we figure out what we're doing."

"That's a good idea."

"Yeah. I try to do smart shit when it counts. But we're getting a little ahead of ourselves. I have to get the job first."

"You'll get it, and they are gonna love you." Savannah touched his face, and she leaned down and kissed his forehead. "They're gonna love you just like I do," she said, and then she realized that she dropped the L word. Savannah looked at Milo.

"Yes, I heard what you said, and yes, it is too late to bring that back now. But not to worry, I've been desperately in love with you since that first day at freshman orientation. I've just been waiting all these years to show you just how much I love you."

"Okay. I've heard how men get funky when you drop the L word on them before y'all are ready to hear it."

"True. But not in this case. In this case, I decided that I was madly in love with you a long time ago."

"You said something about showing me just how much you love me," Savannah said, and that gave them the excuse they needed to make love again.

The following morning, Savannah had Oscar take her to the office, and then he was to take Milo to his interview.

"You should be done with the interview by noon, and we can have lunch together."

"Cool."

When they got to Intuitive Energy, Savannah leaned over and kissed Milo, and since the L word had already been dropped, she felt comfortable saying, "I love you."

"I love you too," Milo said, and Savannah got out of the car. "It's just you and me, Oscar."

"And we are on our way."

When Savannah got to the office, Kiera signaled for her to come into her office.

"What's wrong?"

"Nora Berry and Kristina Byrd were up here earlier today, and they were literally at each other's throats over productivity issues."

"You're kidding." Savannah plopped down in one of the seats in front of Kiera's desk.

"I wish I were. I thought they were gonna come to blows. That's how serious it was."

"What's the gist of it?"

"Nora was saying that Kristina's department was causing productivity losses by doing a combination of inefficient processes, poor tracking, and some other nonsense I didn't get because they were yelling at each other."

"Probably was about incomplete communication, overhead, and onboarding." Savannah stood up. "How'd you leave it?"

"I told them I would express their concerns when you got in. I mean, they were here at five minutes after eight looking for you. Because everybody knows that you get here at a quarter to eight, and they were gonna catch you before you got a chance to do anything else. Anyway, I told them that you would speak to each of them with a solution when you got in." Kiera glanced at her watch. "By the way, why are you late this morning?"

Savannah sat down. "Milo is here. He's got an interview with a company called Insight Innovators."

"Never heard of them."

"Neither have I. Anyway, they sell ergonomic and hammock chairs."

"You two are getting pretty serious if he's looking for a job here."

"He surprised me with it when he showed up this weekend."

"How do you feel about him moving here?"

"I'm all for it." Savannah stood up and turned toward her office. "Let me get settled, and then I'll walk down there and take care of this."

"Have fun."

"Right. I'm just glad they're on different floors."

Once Savannah got settled, she left her office and took her elevator down to see Kristina Byrd. As soon as she saw Savannah come into her unit, Kristina stopped what she was doing and came straight for her.

"Thank you for coming. I swear to God, that woman is crazy."

"Let's go in your office, and you can tell me all about it," Savannah said, patting her on the back to both comfort and calm her down as they walked. Once in her office, Kristina laid out her concerns for Savannah. She listened attentively and nodded when she felt it was appropriate.

"First off, in your position, being who you are"—Savannah pointed to the darker side of her hand—"you cannot, under any circumstance, allow someone to get under your skin to the point where you are in her face ready to come to blows. Sister, do you hear me? Because I'm not fuckin' around here. You were down the hall from Brodrick Fowler's office acting a fool first thing in the morning. I just can't have that. You can't have that."

"I know, Savannah, and I'm sorry. I gotta remember, whether we like it or not, all of us represent all of us. One of us acts a fool, we're all foolish."

"*And you know this.*" Savannah hit her hands with each word. "I know my mother spent years drilling that lesson into me until she was sure I knew it." Savannah shook her head. "She used to say, 'Savannah, you can't do what the white girls do.'"

"Mine too. I just gotta learn to control this temper I got."

"Learn it. Fast. Brodrick is out of the country, so the only one who knows you acted a gotdamn fool on the executive floor is Kiera."

"I'm sorry, Savannah. I promise it won't happen again."

"I know it won't. I can't push you out there if people think you're a fool."

Kristina raised her right hand to testify. "I swear fo' God, it won't happen ever again."

"Same way you gotta talk in white folks' voice, you have to learn to have an 'around white folks' mentality. Every day, someone, somewhere, is going to say or do something stupid in front of you."

"Damn near every minute of every day."

"And, sister, you know this. So what you gotta do is learn to know when to say fuck it."

"What?"

"You heard me. You have to develop the mentality where someone does something that pisses you off, and you know you should be mad about it, but what you have to do is learn to say, 'Fuck it, that is not what I'm here for.'"

"You're right, Savannah. And thank you."

"For what?"

"You didn't have to come down here and talk to me on the real like you're doing."

"Each one reach one. One day, if you stop acting a fool, you're going to have a chance to do this for a young sister. I expect you to be ready to guide her."

"I will."

"Now, there are processes that Lauren and Fynn have been working on and I just approved that will solve all of your concerns with interacting with Nora's department."

"Thank you, Savannah."

When she left the office, Savannah went down two floors to the department that Nora supervised. She was on the phone in her office when she arrived.

"Let me call you back," Nora said when Savannah sat down in the chair in front of her desk. "Good morning, Savannah. Thank you for coming."

"You want to tell me what this morning was all about?"

As she did with Kristina, Savannah listened attentively and nodded when she felt it was appropriate as she laid out her concerns. And when she was finished, Savannah told her the same thing she told Kristina.

"There are processes that Lauren and Fynn have been working on and I just approved that will solve all of your concerns with interacting with Kristina's department."

"Thank you, Savannah. Can you tell me what those processes are?"

"Slack. It has the potential to improve issue response time because your team would have the ability to send a message via Slack and get a response almost immediately."

"That will help."

Savannah stood up.

"That should have been communicated to the unit managers."

Now she wants to tell me how to do my job.

"I felt that it wouldn't be appropriate to communicate a process to the managers when it hadn't been approved." Savannah paused for effect. "Wouldn't you agree with me, Nora?"

"Yes. That wouldn't be appropriate."

"I didn't think so," Savannah said and returned to her office.

When she got there, Kiera told her that Milo was in her office. "Heather called and said he was at the desk, so I went and got him."

"Thank you, Kiera," she said and went into the office.

"Well?"

"I got the job."

"That's great. Congratulations. We definitely have to celebrate."

"When I got there, they thanked me for coming. Said this was just a formality, a meet-and-greet because once they got my resume, they knew I was their guy. Then, they made an excellent compensation package with a combination of salary, commission, insurance, stock options, a gym membership, and a company car."

"Wow. I told you they were going to love you."

"Like you do."

"Yes." Savannah got her purse from the drawer. "Come on."

Savannah went into Kiera's office. "Milo got the job, so we're going to celebrate. You can reach me on my cell if you need me," she said and headed for the elevator with Milo.

That day, Savannah couldn't be happier.

Chapter Twenty-eight

"Good evening, Mr. Fowler. It's Dennis from the front gate."

"Yes, Dennis?" Brodrick asked and glanced at the clock on the wall. It was eleven thirty, and he wondered what Dennis could possibly want with him at this late hour. "What can I do for you?"

"I'm sorry to be bothering you so late at night, but I have a Riley Riviera here to see you."

Riley Riviera? What the fuck does that drunk want?

Riley Riviera was a member of the Intuitive Energy's board of directors. He was what some of the other members of the board and senior management called a diversity member. There was a time fifteen years ago when the board came under fire for basically being a good ole boys club.

And it was true.

There were no blacks and no female members of the board, and definitely no Hispanics, male or female. It was at that point that the diversity program was forced on them, and board members Courtney Murray and Edwin Sharp were forced out. They were replaced by the likes of Riley Riviera, Erica Horne, and Safa Woodard. Board members Angus Ray, Rowan Pennington, Isaiah Mullen, and Brodrick Fowler were given no choice in the matter. It was extremely fortunate for the good ole boys that each of the new board members turned out to be greedy fucks. When they were told how much money they stood to make by going along with the accounting practices scheme, they were all in.

"Well, then. I think you should send Mr. Riviera back so I can see what he wants. Don't you think so?"

"Yes, sir."

"Send him on."

"Yes, sir."

"How's the wife and kids?"

"Doing fine, sir."

When Brodrick hung up the phone with Dennis, he wondered what Riley Riviera could want with him at this hour of the night.

When Riley Riviera arrived at the house, Brodrick was sitting outside on the screened-in porch, waiting for him, with a bottle of Buchanan's Deluxe. When Riviera got out of his limousine, he approached the house. It had become the consensus option that Marilyn Proctor was the whistleblower, and the knives were out for her.

"Good evening, Riley. What brings you out tonight?"

"I got a visit from Marilyn Proctor at my home tonight."

"Isn't she a VP of something at Intuitive Energy?" he asked because he actually had no idea who Marilyn was. He never heard her name until she was named as being the suspected whistleblower.

"She is."

"VP of R&D if memory serves. If I'm not mistaken. Where are my manners? Can I get you something to drink?"

"What you're drinking is fine, Brodrick."

Even though they served on the same board, Riley Riviera and Brodrick Fowler didn't like each other. The only reason that Riviera was there was because Brodrick was the chairman of the board, so he needed to hear this first.

"Help yourself to this Buchanan's Deluxe."

"Thanks. All I need now is a glass."

Brodrick extended his hand toward the two glasses he'd set out to drink from. He didn't know much about Riley, but what he did know was that he was an oil man. Riviera got the glass, filled it with Buchanan's Deluxe, and drank it down. He poured another drink.

"Now you've had your drink. Tell me what's going on with Marilyn Proctor."

"She showed me this email that she sent to your girl Savannah yesterday," he said and handed over the email.

Brodrick read the email aloud. "'Good morning, Savannah. I am reaching out to you because I'm concerned that the debts and losses are being routed into entities formed offshore, and those transactions are not included in the company's financial statement. I'm also afraid that financial transactions between Intuitive Energy and related companies are used to eliminate unprofitable entities.'" Brodrick handed the email back to Riviera. "Has anyone else seen that?"

"To my knowledge, Savannah."

"Do you know what she said to her?"

"To my knowledge, Savannah toed the company line as I did and told her that nothing like that was going on. Then Savannah told her that she should talk to me about her concerns," Riviera said and refreshed his drink. He quickly drank that down and poured another. Brodrick looked on as he poured.

"I'll need to speak with Savannah about what she said to Marilyn."

"I believe you do, Brodrick. Just thought you should hear it from me first."

"You did the right thing. How'd you leave it with Marilyn?"

"Like I said, Savannah toed the company line. She reassured Marilyn that nothing like that was occurring at

Intuitive Energy." Riviera sat back in his chair. "I mean, this is what you told us you hired her for, am I right?"

Brodrick chuckled. He didn't like being questioned about his choice to take a relatively unknown senior VP at BHV and make her president of Intuitive Energy.

"Savannah Ayers has the most beautiful eyes and a power smile. Each time she holds out her hand, the press and the investors line up to eat the food out of the palm of her hand. That's why I hired her."

"You hired her because you thought Savannah Ayers was too stupid to really know what is really going on here."

Here again, Brodrick didn't like being called on his shit, especially from the likes of this drunk DEI member he was forced to take. However, there was one thing he knew for sure.

"Now I need to talk to Savannah."

"Yeah, you do."

"You know Marilyn better than I do. What type of person is she?"

"If you're asking me if she's the type to run to the SEC, I'd say no. But she is the VP of research and development. To me, that means she likes to dig in and sink her teeth into something."

"So, which is it?"

"Truth is, I really can't say. It could go either way."

You're no help.

Brodrick stood up. When he did, Riviera stood up as well.

"Thanks for making the trip," Brodrick said.

"I thought you needed to hear it from me first."

Chapter Twenty-nine

That next morning, Debra Owsley and her associate, Paige Cox, with FBI Agent Jared Clarke standing off to the side, called a press conference at the Securities and Exchange Commission in Washington, DC.

"Thank you for coming. This is just going to be a brief statement. At the conclusion of that statement, I am not going to take any questions." Debra paused before she continued, "At this time, the Securities and Exchange Commission, in conjunction with the white-collar crime division of the FBI, has opened an investigation into the accounting practices at Intuitive Energy. Thank you for coming." Debra left the podium with Paige as the assembled reporters shouted questions.

Brodrick Fowler was traveling in Europe and couldn't be reached immediately for comment. However, Savannah was available for comment, and she made the following statement.

"I had no idea that anything would cause issues with the accounting practices at Intuitive Energy. I was kept out of the financial aspects of the company. My focus was on running the company as its president."

Brodrick was livid about her statement, and as soon as he saw it, he called Savannah.

"Why would you make a statement like that to the press, Savannah?"

"Because it was the truth, Brodrick!"

Savannah had said it in a tone that Brodrick had never heard coming from her before. He was caught off guard and was about to say something in response, but Savannah continued.

"I was systematically and thoroughly kept away from the accounting practices and the financial aspects of the company. I believe intentionally." Savannah snorted. "It was getting to be funny if it weren't so sad. Anytime I would see Duncan in the hall, either he'd turn and go the other way, or he'd whip out his phone as soon as he saw me and pretend to be actually having a conversation for fear of having to talk to me about Intuitive's financial condition."

Brodrick still wanted to say something about the statement Savannah made to the press, but she was well beyond that. Therefore, before he could say anything, Savannah continued.

"That so-called briefing on the financial health of Intuitive Energy was a joke. He showed me a twenty-minute video that I found out later is used for potential investors, and then I had to drag anything else out of him. So, please, do not insult my intelligence and even attempt to tell me that I was not systematically, thoroughly, and intentionally kept away from the accounting practices and the financial aspects of the company."

Since Savannah was right, and she was systematically, thoroughly, and intentionally kept away from the accounting practices and the financial aspects of the company, Brodrick's point about why she made the statement was answered, and all he could do was move on.

"I'll be back in Houston the day after tomorrow, and we'll talk about this then."

"Okay."

"Until then, Savannah, please don't make any more statements to the press. Please."

"It's kind of hard when they've been camped outside with their cameras and microphones since the Securities and Exchange Commission and the white-collar crime division of the FBI opened an investigation into the accounting practices at Intuitive Energy. But my statement will be I have no comment from this point forward." And then Savannah tossed Brodrick a bone to make him feel better about her. "And I am sorry that I made that statement. I was just as blindsided by the investigation as the rest of you," she lied. "So, when those reporters shoved a microphone in my face and asked me to comment—"

"Don't worry about it, Savannah. I'll be back in Houston in a couple of days, and we'll talk about the next steps. But this is bad, Savannah."

"And my statement will be that I have no comment."

"Thank you," Brodrick said, and he ended the conversation.

But he knew that "bad" was an understatement. If the Securities and Exchange Commission and the FBI had anything, he, all of the board of directors, and some of the senior management could be facing large fines and potential prison time.

It was the same for Savannah. She was well aware of the position she was in. She felt she needed to take the steps she took to protect herself and become a whistleblower. It was Savannah and her advisory team's belief that this was her best defense against the potential for large fines and prison time for something she had nothing to do with. Now, Savannah was left to wonder if this was the real reason Tia Richards retired. Could it be she found out about the scheme and they bought her out for her silence? The fact was that Savannah had been locked out of the financial aspects of the business, and she hadn't touched the stock package she had been given as part of her compensation package; therefore, she and her team felt that should be enough to protect her.

When Brodrick returned to Houston, he assembled a meeting of the board members to discuss the investigation. More importantly, what to do about it. They needed to know where the information came from in order to open this investigation. Did they, indeed, have a whistleblower in their midst?

After meeting with the board and ending with more questions than answers, Brodrick went into Savannah's office and sat down.

"What, if anything, did the board decide?"

"We're going to open our own investigation."

"To find out who our whistleblower is?"

When Brodrick nodded, Savannah's thoughts turned to Dylan Christensen. He was the one in the IT department who gave her access to the board of directors' server so she could download the documents that she gave to the Securities and Exchange Commission.

The next couple of weeks were contentious at Intuitive Energy. The bright spot in Savannah's life had been that Milo had started his new job and had moved into a furnished corporate apartment in Houston. Since his arrival as a full-time Houston resident, Savannah had slept in the apartment every night. Milo had been very happy, not only with the new job but also with finally being able to say Savannah was his woman, as he'd always wanted to since the first time he laid eyes on her at freshman orientation at Texas Southern University.

"You can't imagine how good a feeling that is until you experience it for yourself. The shame is that most people never will have the opportunity to be with who they consider the greatest love of their lifetime. The one who got away, so to speak. The feeling is incredible. Just to be in her presence is wonderful and worth all the years I spent without her," Milo told one of his new coworkers.

"You're right. I would give my left hand to have another shot at Angela Hamilton. She's my one who got away. Instead of her, I got what I used to call the consolation prize. But hey, it hasn't been all bad. I'm still married to her, and we have three great kids. But shit, I gotta be honest, I would give it all up for just one more shot."

"Where is she?"

"No clue. And again, to be honest, I'm glad I don't have a clue where she is. I don't search for her on Facebook or Instagram."

"Some people do that for the one who got away. I did. I've always known exactly where Savannah Ayers was and what she was doing. And when I was lucky enough to have to go to Houston, I was lucky enough to walk right into her."

"Because it was meant to be. You and she are supposed to be together."

"Seems that way."

Therefore, Milo was happy, and Savannah was happy with him. However, her situation at Intuitive Energy was getting more complicated with each passing day. And then it happened. They believed that they found the whistleblower.

Brodrick arrived at Intuitive Energy earlier than usual that morning and left a note on Kiera's desk to have Savannah come to his office as soon as she got in. She read the note. Therefore, when Savannah arrived at seven forty-five, Kiera was waiting for her.

"Massa wanna see you."

"What's up?"

"Heather says they know who the whistleblower is."

When Savannah heard that they had found the whistleblower, a cold chill washed over her body. Was she going to walk into Brodrick's office for her own execution? Savannah didn't know. She went into her office and closed the door. She sat at her desk, spun around, looked at her view for what might be the last time, and took out her phone.

"Ciara Reynolds."

"It's Savannah."

"What's up?"

"They say they found the whistleblower."

"Don't panic."

"I'm not going to panic. I've been called to a meeting in Brodrick's office. I am calling myself putting you on notice before I go in there."

"Smart."

"Yeah, well, I try to do smart stuff when it comes to paying the government a large fine and going to jail."

"Call me and let me know what happens."

"I will."

"Good luck."

"Thanks."

Savannah ended the call and put her purse in the drawer.

Kiera asked, "Are we going to have a job when you come back?"

"I don't know. But I got my dancing shoes on if it becomes necessary."

"If not, I could use the mini vacation."

"Me too."

Savannah took her time as she made the walk down the hall to Brodrick's office.

"Good morning, Brodrick," she said and sat down. "You wanted to see me?"

"Yes." He stood up. "Help yourself to coffee and cinnamon buns."

Once Savannah got up and helped herself to coffee and cinnamon buns and sat down, she felt confident that she hadn't been exposed as the whistleblower. However, her thoughts turned once again to Dylan Christensen.

"What's up?"

"We think we found the whistleblower."

Savannah leaned forward and took a bite of her cinnamon bun. "Who is it?"

"We believe that the whistleblower is Marilyn Proctor. We scrubbed the email server, and we found an email that she sent to you."

"Yes. She expressed her concerns that the debts and losses are being routed into entities formed offshore, and those transactions are not included in the company's financial statement. And that financial transactions between Intuitive Energy and related companies are used to eliminate unprofitable entities."

"And you responded, 'Let's have lunch.' What did you tell her over lunch?"

"At the time, I didn't know that she was spot-on with her concerns, but I assured her that wasn't the case. However, I advised her that if she felt strongly about her concerns, she should address them with her supervisor."

"Marilyn took your advice. But we're still convinced that she went to the Securities and Exchange Commission, and they opened the investigation based on that email."

"Has anyone spoken to Marilyn?"

"No. I wanted to talk to you first."

"I see." Savannah stood up. "I have some calls I need to make. So, if we're done here—"

Brodrick waved her on. "Go. Get to work."

Savannah left Brodrick's office and sent Marilyn a text message.

They are going to come at you over the email you sent me expressing your concerns.

Marilyn replied, Understood.

When Brodrick spoke with Marilyn, she told him that she did, in fact, address her concerns with her direct supervisor, board member Riley Riviera. He was able to assure Marilyn that her concerns were unfounded and she had nothing to worry about.

It was deemed that after speaking with Riley Riviera, he successfully allayed her concerns, and Marilyn assured them that she had not contacted either the FBI or the Securities and Exchange Commission. Therefore, the hunt for the whistleblower continued.

As the weeks turned into months and the investigation into the accounting practices at Intuitive Energy continued, tensions were running hot, especially among the members of senior management who were in on the scheme.

Chapter Thirty

It had been six months since the investigation into the accounting practices at Intuitive Energy began. The FBI and the Securities and Exchange Commission called a press conference. Once again, in Washington, DC, Debra Owsley and her associate, Paige Cox, with FBI Agent Jared Clarke standing off to the side, began the conference.

"Thank you for coming. This is just going to be a brief statement. At the conclusion of that statement, I am not going to take any questions." Debra paused before she continued, "We have found sufficient evidence to refer Intuitive Energy to the Justice Department's white-collar crime division for prosecution. At this time, I'll turn it over to FBI Agent Jared Clarke."

"I thank you all for coming. At this time, the FBI has taken the information from the Securities and Exchange Commission, and we will begin our own investigation based on that referral. Once that investigation is complete, it will be decided if formal charges will be brought against members of Intuitive Energy's board of directors and members of senior management."

"Thank you for coming," Debra Owsley said to end the press conference.

While the FBI conducted its investigation, Intuitive Energy declared bankruptcy. The stock price fell to $20 per share. Some thought it was a good deal, and the stock sold well, and its value increased to $22 per share.

Brodrick Fowler said that was proof that the stock would rebound.

However, it wasn't enough to save them. Brodrick Fowler and board of directors members Riley Riviera, Erica Horne, Safa Woodard, and Angus Ray were convicted of conspiracy, fraud, and insider trading. They received twenty years and four months and were ordered to pay a $5 million penalty. Board member Riley Riviera was sentenced to ten years of jail time and ordered to pay a $15 million fine. Board members Rowan Pennington and Isaiah Mullen settled out of court for $21.5 million.

A new board of directors was seated at Intuitive Energy. They reorganized the company and renamed it International Energy with a much more conservative approach to the market. The new board voted to retain Savannah Ayers as president of the new company.

Ciara sat at her favorite restaurant, Palate Pleasures, waiting for Savannah and Thalia to arrive. While she waited, she took a minute to reflect on her relationship with Zack and her experience with Leona Chandler in Saint Barts. Both had changed her in ways that Ciara never thought possible. She often wondered, if it weren't for Zack exposing her to lesbian sex via his porn habit, would she have allowed herself to be seduced by Leona?

Although Ciara said that her experience with Leona satisfied her curiosity, and it had, it did leave her open to new possibilities. Therefore, when Jared, whom she had been seeing off and on during her thug dating time, said that he'd never had a threesome, Ciara said that she was open to it.

Even though Ciara was into her thug dating phase, lately she'd been spending more time with Jared. They were easing into a very comfortable relationship, and that was fine with her.

"Hey, girl," Thalia said as she slid into the booth.

"How are you doing, Thalia?"

"You know me, awesome as always. What's up with you?"

"I have some news to share, but I'm gonna wait until Savannah gets here."

Thalia nodded. "I hear you. That way, you don't have to repeat yourself."

"It's been more than a minute since we all got together. What's up with you?"

"Nothing much. Kids are grown and trying to be out of control—"

"Not on your watch," Ciara chuckled.

"You know I put this iron foot down," she laughed. "But other than that, it's just been business as usual."

And for Thalia, things between her and Cedric had become business as usual. Although she didn't leave him for Dr. Michael Wilkerson, she continued to see other men and wasn't shy about it. After a while, it began to cause friction in the marriage, not for Thalia, but for Cedric. They talked about it, and after a lot of discussion, Thalia was able to show Cedric that it enhanced their relationship and made each appreciate the other.

"Sorry to keep y'all waiting," Savannah said when she arrived at Palate Pleasures.

"No worries," Thalia said. "I just got here. I haven't even gotten a chance to order a drink."

Ciara held up her empty glass. "Well, I've been here long enough to finish this drink."

"That just means that we'll have to catch up," Savannah said and fist bumped with Thalia as their server arrived with menus.

"I don't need a menu. I know what I want," Ciara said.

"She'll have the chicken marsala," Thalia said as she looked over the menu.

"How did you know?"

"It's your favorite comfort food," Savannah said.

"True."

"I'll have the chicken Creole," Savannah said and handed the server the menu.

"And I'll have the grilled teriyaki chicken," Thalia said.

"What are you ladies drinking?"

"Bring us a bottle of your best champagne," Savannah said, and it raised eyebrows with her girls.

"I guess you're not the only one with news to share, Ciara," Thalia said.

"I guess not."

"I didn't want to step on your news," Savannah said. "Go ahead, Ciara. What's your news?" Savannah asked.

"The partners were so impressed with the work I've done and the way I handled Leona Chandler that they gave me another big account to handle."

"That's great," Thalia said.

"Congratulations," Savannah said as their server returned with a bottle of champagne.

"Limited edition Dom Pérignon P2 vintage," their server said, and poured a glass for each.

"That's not all," Ciara said. "I am now officially on the fast track to make partner."

"Now that's something to drink to," Thalia said.

"Congratulations," Savannah said.

"Thank you, thank you," Ciara said, and the three friends drank to it. "Now, Savannah, what are you celebrating?"

"I'm getting married!" Savannah put her left hand on the table to reveal her 2.2-carat certified diamond three-stone engagement ring in fourteen-karat white gold. "Milo asked me to marry him, and I said yes."